THE ANTIPODE ROOM

AN AUSTRALIAN FUGUE NOVEL

Books by Ruth Skilbeck

Australian Fugue Series
Australian Fugue: The Antipode Room a novel
The Antipode Room a novel illustrated with art images
Sayonara Baby a novel
Missing a novel (abridged edition of *Australian Fugue*)
Sayonara Baby: Fragments of Memory Images photographic
images and brief excerpts from the Australian Fugue novels

Musico-literary studies
*The Writer's Fugue: Musicalization, Trauma and Subjectivity in
the Literature of Modernity*

~~~

Anthology and Journal
Escape Artists Anthology 2013-2017 editor-in-chief
Arts Features International editor-in-chief

Preface writer & book designer
A Letter From Manus Island by Behrouz Boochani translated
by Omid Tofighian, preface by Ruth Skilbeck
A Brief Guide to Middle Class Homelessness by Kenneth
Wolman, preface by Ruth Skilbeck

RUTH SKILBECK
THE ANTIPODE ROOM

AN AUSTRALIAN FUGUE NOVEL

WITH IMAGES BY THE AUTHOR

BORDERSTREAM BOOKS

New edition first published by Borderstream Books in 2023
Borderstream Books
Whittington, VIC, 3219
www.borderstreambooks.com.au

A catalogue record for this book is available from the National Library of Australia

ISBN: 9780645842210 (paperback)

Cover art: *Blue Fugue* (2013) by Ruth Skilbeck

Cover design: adapted from a design by Maxim Skilbeck-Porter for the paperback first edition of *Australian Fugue: The Antipode Room*.

Designed and typeset by Ruth Skilbeck in Adobe Garamond Pro 12/15 and Helvetica Neue

Contents

FUGUE

English

n. 1. *music,* polyphonic composition in which one or two subjects, melodic phrases, are introduced by one voice and taken up by others. 2. *psychology,* flight from or loss of awareness of self-identity involving the subject wandering away from home, rare response of transitory dissociation following shock or emotional stress.

[F., from It. from Latin: flight]

French

n. 1. wandering impulsion. 2. running away. 3. *fugue amoureuse,* elopement. 4. *fugue romantique,* romantic fugue.

Time's glory is to calm contending kings,
To unmask falsehood, and bring truth to light.
—Shakespeare, *The Rape of Lucrèce*

Madame Flying Doctor's Fugue Notebooks

This is the first Fugue Notebook.

When first I began my research into the mysterious condition of psychogenic fugue—diagnosed as loss of awareness of self-identity coupled with a wandering journey away from Home—I had no idea where it would lead me. I was young and driven; it was years before I earned my stripes. Madame Flying Doctor has come to stand for doctors without borders and Aboriginal flying spirit doctors for flights of healing powers, in many forms. If there are some things that seem fantastical and fictional, this is because some truths we cannot express in any other way. What some of the most visionary artists grasp and see in their dreams and realize in their works, years later becomes a mainstream understanding.

The Antipode Room presented here is the first in the series of Fugue Notebooks.

The Antipode Room is a consulting room, a room for reflection, a mirror fugue, its lines have no stopping points, endlessly looping, repeating, infinite; like Bach's last unfinished fugue, it's a game many can join in and play, a musical round of potentially infinite polyphony, multiple voices. I had no idea when I first entered that box of mirrors, on that raining London day years ago, of the significance of the order of voices, the need for precision, as the precise arrangement of notes in the melody line, is key. I did not know what I do know now about the practical and supra-worldly applications of the fugal modality that speaks in the hidden code of computer binaries, that through the power of alignment can take us to the higher dimension of global human consciousness, set us free. I was fumbling towards infinity, yet I had an intuition that I followed blindly, knowing somehow… It is the work of the artist to decide when it stops. It is the work of the fugue doctor to decide where it starts.

Fugue in Medical Discourse
The questions associated with phenomena of psychogenic fugue identified in recent and current medical/psychiatric discourse are to do with the subjective nature of memory, consciousness, and personal identity. These issues concern subjective awareness and loss of awareness of the self. These are areas of ambiguity in Philosophy of Mind, and Phenomenology, that have long provided 'questions with no answers' for philosophers. These problems have eluded empirical medical knowledge. Considering contexts of the subject's life is a holistic approach considered by K who said to better understand the phenomenon of psychogenic fugue, we must understand the subject's life context and experience.
K conducted intensive research into case studies, which seek to understand social, cultural, and individual personal dimensions of the psychogenic fugue narrative.

Note
Names of characters have been made up where information is missing and the investigation is underway.

Prelude

Young woman alone
Playing violin
Falling dusk
Darkening room

'I've got Bach's *Art of Fugue*. I can put that on. I often listen to it when I'm going to sleep. It's my bedtime music,' she adds suggestively.

She half sits up and leans over me. The top of her Japanese robe falls open.

She leans and touches the player beside the bed.

The first slow haunting bars of the fugue, the searing profound beauty of a solo violin shatters the still warm arm.

Suddenly she twists. She kisses me on my lips. This is the last thing that I want.

I wanted the love of my life that she stole away from me.

And that's when it happens.

That's when everything went red.

A fireball exploded at the back of my head with a blinding impact of noise—blood—spurting over her, over me.

And then nothing.

From faraway a bell is ringing. Ringing, ringing. Ringing. Boring into my brain.

I open my eyes, and rise from the bed like a sleepwalker...

Every morning I wake in hope. I've heard that amputees forget their limb's not there. Feeling a phantom limb. All I saw, heard in my dreams, were ghosts.

I remember the blood, red, I had a pain in my head. I hear the dawn chorus, bird's first melodies. See black, white, verticals. Bars, light, bars. Hear warders shouting. Rattling doors.

See an aeroplane fly by, a pale frail amoeba swimming in infinity. My window to reality, the outside world, is striped. Prison grids it.

And I shall tell Doctor. No.

Enlightenment, which I long for, did not illuminate my dreams, again. I did not remember in the night.

And I will move through this day, as the past four hundred and thirty. A life sentence ahead. Following my trial. Someone did it. But who? The full moon rises each month, drowns me in seductive grief. If I am good, they say I will be allowed to paint. I am good. My good work is my offering, chicken's blood, and palm oil. Tap-tap-tap. Keep on going as I try to recall, the murder which led to my conviction.

The murder I cannot remember.

Tap-tap-tap, my fingertips press the keys of the laptop Sir Hugo brought before he returned home, which they let me keep in my cell. I'm trying to reconfigure that Time blanked from my mind. What happened? Throw myself on the narrow bed...

Bach was a master of the art of fugue...

Her words repeat, a code I'm struggling to crack.

4

It's my bedtime music.

Repeating, infernal internal Nietzschean CD track, stuck on eternal return.

Did he? Did she? What happened? I don't know. But I was supposed to have been there! I must remember, so I will be able to forget. Move on, at least, figuratively speaking. To move on out of here, a free woman would be bliss. Divine.

Forget. Her violent violin. Lay to rest, my nemesis.

Haunted for so long.

Remember. Margarita, swooping, soaring. Flying, falling. Cutting the still air of the Castle into bittersweet motifs, ribbons and confetti, with the geometry of her bowing arm.

Dancing to her music, in a blood red gypsy dress.

You'll get it, the missing real-to-reel.

Talk-it-up. Talk-out. Roll up for the five-dollar-a-minute talking cure. Here it's on the house. The counsellors, shrinks, doctors, say. Think. And you will find. That missing piece. Is buried deep within. Lost behind a couch, perchance? Hugo's chaise longue that Demeter, my delightful mother-in-law, said had once belonged to Oscar Wilde.

Under a bed, maybe? Hugo's bed or Ray's…he was always the untidy one when he was out-of-order.

That long-lost bit of me that will, that might, see me free.

I want to find the one I am searching for.

Bring her back from the Other Side.

What did Father Aristotle say without a seeming trace of irony in the prisoner chapel service last Sunday? The truth, my sisters, the Truth will set you free.

The last thing I remember clearly is preparing to go to Australia to collect art for my gallery.

Day Six

Ruby

Ruby Love Gallery, London, December 6, 2001

BANG!

Ouch! Sounds of industry crash against my hangover. Susan and Ham are renovating the Antipode Room ready for our return from Australia, laden with art and contracts if all goes to plan. Fresh blood, to inject colour and vitality into the antipodean collection I'm becoming known for.

I aim to stir up the artworld. Make something happen. Waste swamped art this fin-de-millennium. Doug & Dan's excremental exhibition drew the highest audiences ever on record in the history of the Royal Academy. Am I the only gallerist in town craving visions to inspire us? Though I won't let anyone know. Authentic, cutting-edge, as it undoubtedly is.

'Ruby! Must you exhibit abjection, my dear?' Sir Hugo joked as I helped hang the show.

'Cheer up! Be happy! Celebrate life!!'

It was Hugo's idea that we go. He's been persuading me to take him for years since soon after we pledged our troth. Going to my 'homeland' as Hugo teasingly refers to it is not something I thought I could do. I have a lingering idea that I came from there, but scant memory of my family, that was all lost in the Accident. I agreed because I know it's what the Gallery needs now. It's a business trip. That's all.

Blearily I pick up photocopies from my desk. On the top is an image framed by text, an island of tranquillity floating amidst a sea of words that swim and melt before my eyes.

I force myself to look, as if it will make me feel better. The image is grainy, reduced, diminished, rendered in shades of grey, a faded memory of itself, but intriguing magic shimmers through.

I look at delicately painted images. Chinese women semi-clad in loose robes, enclosed in small rooms. Accompanying each one is a different type of bird.

Who are the beauties, are they courtesans? What does the title mean *Beauties Captured in Time*? I flick open a catalogue; find a colour image. The work, by the Chinese-Australian artist, Wang Zhiyuan, is based on the ancient folk style of colour print, and picture albums destroyed at the beginning of the Qing dynasty, the remaining ones banned in the Cultural Revolution, I read.[1]

My eye is seized by the vivid vermilion of the background against which the painted women's skin shines. Deep crimson so deliciously deep I could drink it. I'd like to drape myself in its velvet depths, curl up and hide inside it. Live suspended eternally within it, like the beauties...

My stomach surges threateningly. Elbows on desk, rest my face in my hands. Leaning on the Beauties, close my eyes.

Despite diazepam, my head is pounding. I'm sure there was a time when I did not have to keep up with Hugo and cronies, the alcoholic academics; I (privately) term them. I'd have two, three glasses of wine, no more, but lately I've been drinking to almost keep pace with Hugo, and that's a feat. I even get a sick kick from the wasted nausea, hammered-brain pain of an all-day hangover. For which I've found the cure is a drink (after 6 p.m., there's no harm, I tell myself). Another drink, another, then a snort or two and I'm in a crystal prism, spinning colours radiating from thoughts, and every wisp of dream appears real, brilliant, and true, until I stand up and almost fall flat on my face.

If I were an artist, not the gallerist that I am, I would have stayed up all last night, painting, I was jittery, restless with a yearning tug in the depths of my being, pulling me to an unknown point I have to burst out from. At home I didn't feel at home, as I walked through the shiny yellow front door of Rivers Chase terrace in Primrose Hill, which has been in Hugo's family for a century. I couldn't stop pacing the rooms, fidgeting. Rearranging flowers, straightening photographic artworks on flock-papered walls, I even began to fossick in the cupboard beneath the stairs, looking for the vacuum.

I forced myself to stop; I was going out with Hugo—dinner at the Vienna on the Strand with several of his colleagues. Changing outfits, decisions… My thigh high leather boots or kitten-heel Mangle's—and if so, which ones?

With half an eye to the Gallery's reputation I entertained the company with whimsical theories of art I think they've come to expect from Hugo River's young wife. So I shocked them with the Phi-Love Room. As if from a distance I heard my voice curling archly around the words recounting what I'd written about in *Planet Art*.

"Phi' is a drug derived from phenylethyl-amine, which has a similar chemical configuration, apparently, a stimulant, apparently, fills imbibers with ecstatic love and sexual energy.'

'Is it?' Professor Brian Bear raised his bushy eyebrows.

'Ruby!' Esmé exclaimed. 'How do you know this?'

'A European artist made an installation called the Phi-Love

Room. Participants take 'phi', then climb into swinging 'love harnesses' to indulge in a clever reference to Fragonard's *The Swing.'*

'Love it! Love his work! Had a copy of the dress made up for me, all that pink satin mmm scrumptious!' Esmé giggled.

'The eighteenth-century painting of a young lady dressed in voluminous masses of pink soaring on a swing pushed by her priest, her leg is raised and her shoe flies, symbol of loss of virginity, as a young nobleman reclining in the bushes before her has a view up her skirt.' Recalled from my essay verbatim.

'You know,' said Esmé, 'I wore it to Brian's ceremony.'

'It represented scandalous frivolity, exploitation of women and aristocratic decadence, religious corruption. All that was supposedly *wrong* with the Ancien Régime before the French Revolution.'

As I spoke I looked at her and raised my eyebrows.

'Do you see it like that? I just love the picture.'

Esmé nibbled her crème caramel.

Politely raucous laughter from the gentlemen. Hugo puts his hand on my thigh under the table...

'You're joking,' said Rufus, Ethics lecturer, looking slightly alarmed. 'Naughty, making things up to entertain us.'

'It's true, Jasper Jackson plans to give it a whirl next time he's in Cologne...'

Laughing over sherries by the fireside with Sir Hugo last night... Laughing because I can't stop what I've started...

Acting as if everything is perfectly under control. Playing a part, married to the older philosopher, playing in the London art world as if born to it.

But why I wonder in my calmer, more reflective moments, typified by a hangover, like now, renovation banging shaking my spine, staring at the sleeting rain in Charlotte Walk, why is it so much easier to play a role than to live life authentically, be yourself, be real? And what does it mean to 'be real'? Know thyself is a Greek proverb. But how can you know thyself, what is Self? Answer this Jean-Paul, I ask the ghost of existentialism. There are no answers only questions... He says, just like Hugo.

But I think I must be good at it. Reinvention. Whichever way you want to spin it, if you don't know, or can't remember, who you are, if at heart you are nobody to yourself, so long as you keep on living as if you are somebody, it's enough. Who bluffs best, wins? Isn't that what it's all about, in society? It's developed into a principle by which I live my life.

My eighteenth-century writing desk in the room we call the 'mistress bedroom' conceals a file folder in which I keep articles on a condition that fascinates me. Last night when I couldn't sleep, I rose, and crept down the passage that joins the master bedroom to the mistress. I seized the manilla folder and read a strange, familiar story.

In the drawer of the desk are press clippings about Hugo and me from the art press and society pages, in which our names are writ in bold letters.

ART ARISTOCRACY WEDDING

COUNTESS RUBY CUTS THE CAKE

In the drawer are portfolios of art journalism stories. After we opened Ruby Gallery I stopped writing journalism, though I write occasional essays for Art. I concentrate on selling works judiciously, discreetly, to discerning collectors.

According to the media we are a perfect partnership. High profile couple! Agenda-setting gallerist, and contrarian philosopher! But nobody knows Hugo like I do. And nobody knows who I am.

Nobody knows the dreams, half-memories, thoughts that rise like dark waves threatening and ominous in the back of my head in the dead of night, terrifying quiet.

Nobody knows about the phantoms that play inside my head. Last night as I lay beside Hugo spinning-out with the after-effects of champagne and my after-dinner snorts in the Ladies at Vienna, in my mind I saw the tidal wave, tsunami, gathering in darkness with all the power of everything I have lost, forgotten.

'Antipodes is Greek for 'having the feet opposite.' I'll have a sign in the Antipode Room, saying that, a definition,' I said to Hugo as I drove him to work this morning.

'The antipode is the point at which the diametric relation is measured, which you would reach on the other side of the world if you drilled in a straight line all the way through the earth and came out at the other side, and vice versa.'

'Yes,' he assents as I speed across the Euston intersection.

'Australians are often called 'antipodean'. But the antipode point of England is not in Australia but in the South Pacific Ocean about four hundred miles east of the east coast.

If 'antipodean' designates a relation rather than fixed point of origin shouldn't that mean that in Australia England is the antipodes?'

'You're joking!' He threw back his head and laughed.

I winced and accelerated through an amber light, to turn into Torrington Place.

Oh Rose thou art sick/The invisible worm/That flies in the night/In the howling storm:/ Has found out thy bed [2]

I might have known it. That poem's been on my mind for weeks. It's worse than having a ditty from the radio repeating in your mind. At least that's normal, a hazard of inner-city life. Living in a marketing web, some of its jingle jangles are bound to, irritatingly, lodge in your ears. But having a poem stuck on random replay is a different matter. A poem that's imprinted itself in a forgotten memory migrating into your consciousness of its own volition has to make you ask, why?

Where did it come from? What could it mean?

...found out thy bed/Of crimson joy:/And his dark secret love/ Does thy life destroy [3]

The sick rose, rain, banging, dark December sky, it all pounds around me. The dull overload of a diazepam-soothed hangover. I took a tab when I reached the gallery, and feel removed from the morning as if I'm in a blood-temperature cocoon.

This morning I sold two works. Received a cheque for a sum in the mail. Ruby is going well, very well. We're collecting, we're expanding, making a profit in difficult times. We're about to go to Australia. I have nothing to worry about. Everything to celebrate, enjoy. As Hugo keeps saying, but he's right. He's always been right. Unlike me. Hugo was born right.

Susan approaches staggering beneath a box from the back room. She puts it on the floor beside me, and we sift through the heaps of papers that have piled up in boxes. Catalogues, reviews. Even a clipping about Admiral's Emeralds, the racehorse Hugo owned. All must be disposed of to make space for the collection of antipodean art.

'File, file, throw,' I say as she holds up items to my scrutiny.

Then, 'What about these?' My assistant holds up a photo

envelope. It looks suddenly, wrenchingly, familiar. I hold out my hand. What is this? Who are these photos of? What are they doing here? The numbing effect of the diazepam dissipates. Be still my beating heart. I force shock into cynicism. Pull out the first photo, staring at it with a willed immunity.

The image of the blue sky is dazzling, radiant. It's high summer in the High Country of New South Wales. In my hand I am holding a young woman. She is dancing around the side of the weatherboard farmhouse, wearing a black silk slip, holding her skirt in an ironic curtsey, parodying a country girl. Heidi smiling at her goatherd. She is wearing a bee-keeper hat with a long green veil. Laughing.

The next image is a close-up. The same girl peeping with a dramatic expression, black eyelashes accentuate deep blue eyes. Her arms held in balletic third position, left arm curved, the other extended, head tilted back like a model from the 1950s. I am momentarily transfixed by the exquisite refinement of her expression. She is acting, yet in the act, a hidden side of herself is revealed or made up, but who can tell?

I select a third photo. The same girl in a farmhouse kitchen. Playing violin. Wearing the same black silk dress. Ebony curls spill over her shoulders.

Fourth photo. A young man wearing a straw hat standing with a young woman who looks disturbingly familiar. They are next to the farmhouse veranda; the steps are not visible but are apparent in different levels of their elevation. She is on the top step; hair pulled up in a ponytail reveals high cheekbones. Her expression is pensive. A girl from another world, gazing into an inner space. Caught in three-quarter profile she is in shadow, brooding. In contrast, the image of the young man is bleached by the sun. His face is white, overexposed. As is his nude torso. A backpack slung over his shoulders. He is looking with a provocatively blank expression at the photographer.

My imagination whirs.

Who are they? Was he setting out on an expedition, in the backpack were there watercolours, sketchbooks, and inks? Was he an artist? Was she?

'Bloody hell.' I hear the sharp tone and choice of expletive as if the words are coming from someone else's mouth.

Fanning the photos, I replace them in the envelope.

'Throw these out.'

Susan is squatting on the floor. In calico pyjamas, with her head shaved, why she would want to adopt such a look in the middle of an English winter is beyond me.

She looks at me curiously.

'Is everything alright?' She asks.

'Where did these come from?'

'The back room, the Antipode Room,'

As she reaches over, I involuntarily pull back, tuck the flap down, hurling the photos into the box: to join a precipice of resumés, multi-dimensional curricula vitae, taped biographies, public relations hype, applications from artists wanting to show in the gallery. Flick. Forget. Without a further thought.

As if it really were that easy.

Rain beats, drums, against walls of windows, walls of glass that protect me from the streets, from the cold, hunger, greed, the needs of people who look the way I used to look and feel, on the streets in the pouring rain. After I 'came around' on the Northern Line. Re-born like a character in a black-and-white film, joining the Foreign Legion 'to forget.'

Before I met Hugo.

O Ruby thou art sick...[4] I look at the watch Hugo gave me

14

for a birthday. My birthday that —he doesn't know—I decided upon. The eighth of July 1968.

At one-o-clock, in half an hour, I shall meet my Professor for lunch in a whole food restaurant between the Gallery and Princes College.

Lunching at Sprouts is our main health habit. Apart from leisurely Sunday afternoon constitutionals on Primrose Hill. The occasional strolls farther afield into Regents Park, along the canal. To 'shake out cobwebs' as Hugo puts it. Move booze and nicotine through the bloodstream a bit faster would be more accurate, especially on Sunday afternoons. Hugo's capacity for fine wine and tobacco inspires awe. He loves intoxication, although of course he'd never do anything illegal. Hugo likes to stay firmly within the limits of the law, and in his role as Ethical Adviser to government, he's well-rewarded for his love of authority—which I know about intimately.

When I started living with Hugo I was intrigued, amused, and a little carried away by what it conferred: the novel sense of power, and well-being, it bestowed. He was well dressed, quite the dandy in his bespoke suits, and perfectly fitted hand-made shoes. A philosopher. After we married I enjoyed the challenges of living in luxury and privilege and running the gallery he gave me as a wedding gift. Until—what? The 'thing-in-itself' set in. It's been three years, the golden egg has started to lose its lustre, and I can hear it starting to crack.

Susan turns on the heel of her work boot and walks out of my office, dripping papers. The pale floorboards shake with her footsteps. Through the open doorway I can hear her and Ham the manager; the muted buzz of voices shattered by more banging.

A woman in green is peering intently at the series Nuclear

Family, Still Life With Mushroom Cloud. My torpor sustained through the morning's business deals has disappeared. *The invisible worm/ That flies in the night/ In the howling storm...*[5]

The thought of those photos is disturbing me, the images familiar-distant like a name on the tip of one's tongue.

The prospect of going there is making me nervous, jumpy, and I've slipped into a secret self-destructive coke and diazepam habit in addition to Hugo' s booze, to try and deal with it all.

Back in that landscape of beauty and terror... In six days time... It's almost impossible to believe...I tell myself it's just another business trip. Every month Ruby goes on trips. No different just because it's 'Australia.' It must be years since I was last there. It might as well be another country, a Republic, dictator state, Shangri-La, for all the effect it will have. Anyway, I'm going to be so busy there won't be time to do anything but business as I have been trying to explain to Hugo who seems to want it to be a special sort of 'holiday.'

From the corner of my eye I can see the rubbish box. The envelope fell open as I threw it. I can see an edge of the silver farmhouse roof. My resolve wavers. I want to look at the photos again, to scrutinize them in private. Interrogate their faded surfaces; it's ridiculous. I've thrown them out. Ruby get on with it. I admonish myself. I'm good at that. Admonishing myself. And getting on with work. That's how come I'm here now, sitting in the Director's chair.

To me, the practice of efficiency is thrilling; I got off on its subliminal power charge. At least I tried. The style fetishisation of business from the cut of suits to the right kind of pen, and laptop. At that point in my life I had not thought it might be oppressive as if it were the bargain we are com-pelled to make to enter culture on equal terms, considered acceptable and accepted only if we appear right, and act out the subtly (or otherwise) fetishised or romanticised styles in the mass media, surrounded by 'role models' like not-so-secret secret agents of desire. Today I was wearing a bright red, low-cut corset dress, turquoise necklaces, black leather boots. My hair in loose curls.

Before me: images by Rhett Felix. Belle. Burudyara. A 'Bad artist', 'landscape painter', 'cultural historian', according to the descriptions. Artists whom I hoped to collect on the trip. I stare at Burudyara's word sculpture RAPED. On a better day I might feel inclined at this point, the low ebb before lunch to go into my office. Browse my collections, allow myself to fall into the images like dreams. Objects, I can hold within my gaze, possess in a way impossible to possess a real lover. Make mine forever.

Losing myself in art energises, revitalises me. Puts a spring in my step, winning sparkle in my patter, the polish Hugo adores: Talk to me like I'm a client, Ruby, show me the prints. I smile at the memory, an expression of entreaty on his pale, taut, handsome face.

But this morning despite success of business deals, instead of feeling efficient, and excitingly in control, I feel dizzy. Head spinning, heart racing, a high-pitched ringing in my left ear.

Is my eardrum bursting? O God, panic surges through my veins. I press fingertip to ear, sounded like it was coming from above, perhaps connected to the renovations, now it sounds like it's in my head instead. Ruby, you're panicking, baby, that's all it is. Recently, the panic attacks have been frequent. That's what Doctor M. calls this sense of racing dissolution, the-end-of-the-world mortal terror that grabs me onto its black back and bolts down a flying track to swerve on a curve of calamity, the end. 'Panic attacks'. I do what doc suggests. Take out a paper bag from a desk-drawer, hold it over my mouth and breathe deeply. I look at the colours, and tangles of lines, focusing on my breathing as I've learnt in yoga class.

Slowly the ringing-sound abates; the whirling vortex, my tangled vision, coalesces into tangible images. I can see what it is I'm looking at. I stand up slowly, carefully. Three minutes ago, a nervous wreck. Now calm enough to handle objects.

My ankle-length black coat with faux-fur trim is hanging on the coat-rack in my office. I slip into its folds, pick up my umbrella.

Looming in my field of vision, that rubbish box. I just can't seem to keep it out of my sight. Very soon, when I'm at lunch, the box will be thrown into the bins behind the gallery. Taken away down the River Thames in a barge. Seagulls will peck with sharp orange beaks.

Photographs...

I pick up my Kernel clutch bag. Looking at the image of the violinist. A ghostly, ethereal music obsessed her.

Her face quivers with that expression of sweet intense private pain that she gives herself to when she plays alone, believing herself unseen. I hover in the shadows of the French doors. Inadvertently spying on her; I remind myself of those scary vengeful-looking girls in paintings by her favourite artist, images of intense, huge-eyed daughters whom she adores. She doesn't notice me; too far-gone. Swooping-soaring on high-pitched sound. She plays a wrong note. Patiently, obsessively, flicking back black locks she starts again.

Forget it I tell myself, but then something else takes over. I let myself go. In my state of daydream, an extraordinary thing happens, the ringing is increasing in intensity, pitch, reaching a crescendo so my brain feels like it's going to burst. Instead the ringing bursts out, breaks, into the sweetest music of a choir of high-pitched angelic voices. The image and choral sound fuse together in a swoon of violent longing.

I bend, and snatch the photo envelope from the rubbish box. The gallery is unusually quiet. As I am straightening up, Susan's booted footsteps break the silence. I slide the photographs into my bag. My hands shake, three spill on the floor. I pick them up.

Turning, I give Susan my director's gaze.

'I'll be back this afternoon. If anyone calls.'

'Okay, boss,' she looks me in the eyes, as if she thinks there is something a little odd about me. That's the problem. I never know whom I should trust, if anyone. Probably no one.

'Oh, and Susan', I look meaningfully at her pyjamas. 'It's the Antipode Room, not the Convict Room.'

'You what?'

I smile, and exit through the doorway without freezing or falling. Put up my umbrella and walk in the light icy rain.

Hugo

Princes University College

I was magnetically attracted to Ruby from the moment I first saw her. At introductory drinks for students on the new evening course. She arrived late. Or, I should say, she made an entrance.

The room was crowded. My eyes swung across the bodies, faces, as the needle of a compass meets north. She was standing in the doorway. Red-gold tresses cascaded to her waist, and, miracle, she was wearing a fur coat.

In an age of hunt saboteurs, animal rights, she stood out like Wanda in *Venus in Furs*, awe-inspiring amongst peers in parkas. Nerve. She was extraordinary, commendable.

My eyes met hers with a jolt that set my nerves alight. I did not have much of an understanding of Plato's theory of the meeting of souls until that moment, but the thrill of recognition when I gazed at the striking bronze-haired woman and she looked back made me sympathetic to Plato's concept of love. That each soul is split at birth and henceforth roams the earth searching for its soul mate. My eyes held hers for what seemed like an eternity. I will never forget the moment. I remember now with longing…Soon she wove through the milling throng, holding out a glass towards a bottle of champagne that I, as welcoming professor, was jovially dispensing; laughing with a charm that made me feel years younger.

I did not mention her fur coat on that evening, but later as the year progressed, we became intimate, she confided to me that she bought it in a second-hand shop as it was cheap.

'Only ten pounds can you believe and twice as much for

old raincoats that looked as if they'd come straight off a flasher's back.' One quality I appreciate in my wife is refinement. Unlike many young women of my acquaintance, she knows when to stop. Never goes too far into areas of tastelessness, vulgarity. She's as restrained, self-controlled, filled with decorum as the Splendid Women I read about contorting their bodies in elevated states of consciousness.

And if she lacks energy sometimes that suits me too. After all, physique is not as it was. Our shared faith and devotion to the work ethic to which one sublimates baser desires suits me fine in a woman. I find it more than admirable. And I want to reward her with lavish gifts for the way in which she controls me, every night in masquerades.

I have given her precious jewels. Emeralds for eternity.

The first time we made love she was wearing her fur coat. I asked her. Every time I saw her in it afterwards I was reminded of the moment of union, the blissful merging of bodies and soul. After which I asked her—to be my wife.

With sweetly lowered eyes, touching modesty, she agreed.

She wore her fur for quite a while. She wore it everywhere.

Despite jeers of girls who followed her on the street asking if she'd kill a mink, a fox, her own dog. She told me that she'd turned and said she'd bought it in a charity second-hand shop. She couldn't afford one of their leather bags! The reason she bought it was because it was cheap. Fur coats had lost value, she knew why, like them she was opposed to slaughter of animals but she had to stay warm or would herself become extinct.

Not afraid to be herself, my Ruby Love.

In that way we are truly soul-mates.

She ceased wearing her fur when she could afford to buy

something warm yet uncontroversial, wool and stylish tweeds. The woolly fleece woven into threads, rather than the leather or furry hide of backs and sides of the beasts, but she'd made her point with me.

I rescued her fur coat a while ago; it was in the rubbish bin. She'd thrown it out. I cleaned off scraps of food, and brought it back inside, it's in my wardrobe now, concealed behind a row of suits. Every now and then I take it out, stroke its softness, drape it over my shoulders, and wrap it as far as it will go around my torso. Regard my reflection in the mirror.

One night, I'll surprise her.

I'll bring out her proud pelt and insist that she wears it— like she did the first time.

Ruby

Streets of Bloomsbury

When I'm on my way to meet Hugo it comes back. As I'm walking past windows sprayed with snow. Grief I could hide. Pretend it didn't exist, I felt all right. I could forget white rooms, the last sensation as I disappeared under anaesthetic, the angel behind my shoulder; she'd been there for weeks. When I re-emerged the angel was gone. It was just I, alone. Much too alone. Forget all that. What I couldn't forget. I couldn't escape the pain, or prevent the fainting fits.

After 'arriving' in London I moved into a rented room in a house in Camden which I'd seen advertised on a notice board in a shop, a couple of days after I came around.

I still don't know what I did when I crash landed in London. I must have slept in a park; the clothes I wore were crumpled, unwashed, bits of grass and twig in my hair. I did find a plane ticket in my bag, which is how I thought I came from Sydney; the date of arrival on the ticket had been three days prior. The bag held documents, a leather purse filled with dollar notes. I slept that night in a hostel in Euston, and converted the cash. After I moved into the house, I realized my nausea exceeded a pure existential reaction to the shock of my fugue and exile.

I was alone, a stranger without friends, no family here, nor money. No means of help, nor job although I planned to look for work in galleries around Camden. I'd been too numbed to do anything. On an unconscious level I had made a decision to forget. Forget him, forget her; everything that led to my flight. But my body didn't want to forget. My body wanted to celebrate lost love with a gift of new life. It was doomed, and deformed from the start.

I had three hundred pounds, enough to cover and tide me over. I felt life gushing away in agonizing tangible form. Bodies make metaphors and my body was sobbing and screaming with pain of loss.

I had to pull myself together. Or else I would disintegrate in that red river, dissolve in the flow of blood. Disappear into nothingness, hollow empty madness of void that loss, that triple loss, left inside me. Life, the future, and the child not born. I could not think about it. Each month I was reminded with mocking regularity.

I watched Veronika Voss fascinated by the steel will and somehow, strangely, erotic work ethic of Hanna Schygulla's Voss. In tightly tailored business suits, stream-lined efficiency, Veronika stayed up into the early hours with just a coffee cup, balancing her books. She was on a mission to transform her life.[6]

No matter that *Get Out*'s film critic said Voss represented Germany's trials after the Third Reich. After achieving 'impressive' results from efficiency she accidentally blew up herself, her apartment, and entire apartment building, in a misjudged attempt to light a cigarette from a gas stove.[7]

I didn't want to do that but, I asked myself, if I work hard, harder than I'd ever thought, might I escape into a weightless future; escape the past? Could I create a new life for myself?

I started work as assistant curator at the Body of Work Gallery in Camden, and began writing artist profiles for London's listings magazines, and national newspapers. I was just about making ends meet because I wasn't paying rent. I'd met Kat, a singer in a nightclub and moved into her elegant dilapidated Georgian terrace squat near Regent's Park; living with a group of musicians, artists, cycle-couriers, Giles, a merchant banker and his friend Tom, a defence scientist, fashion students and artists.

'There's thousands of homeless people yet thousands of properties left empty, it's an open invitation to squatters.' Kat had shouted in my ear, as we shimmied to *Venus in Furs,* at Alice's in Soho.

'Anarchy rules, man.'

Two years after I first came around in London I enrolled to study Aesthetics, and that's where I met Professor Hugo Rivers, my first year tutor.

The day before my tutorial I passed out in a shop. I was walking down the road from the squat to buy fruit for breakfast. Sudden agonising pains lacerated my chest, could hardly breathe. By the time I reached the shop all I could see was black, white, grainy, disappearing. I was blacking out.

'You alright love?' Vaguely aware of Gerry who owned the

fruit shop. I begged, 'I must lie down.' Voices, muted, buzzing. 'There's nowhere…' 'Sit here.' 'Ambulance?' 'A pound of bananas please.' 'The back steps?' An Asian man was standing beside me taking my pulse.

I was taken by ambulance, lifted up by stretcher and taken to hospital where I stayed for several hours until I recovered. Kat came to collect me in a cab. The medical verdict? 'Painful periods.' The middle-aged doctor peered over his pince-nez. Well, I could have told him that.

'It's rare,' he added. 'But at the onset of the menstrual period the cervix can contract leading to pain and fainting fits.'

'It's only been like this since I had a procedure two years ago,' I said suddenly feeling desperate.

'Can't help you with that,' he closed a file folder and turned his back disapprovingly.

'I'm not a specialist.'

I rang to apologize for missing my tutorial.

'I was taken ill,' I chose the phrase in what I thought was a Darwinian manner, adapt and survive. Or, when in Rome do and say as the Romans. That was how I consciously chose my words.

'Oh.' There was a pause, then: 'Nothing serious I hope?' His bass voice in its velocity and volume was strangely reassuring.

'I passed out in a shop.'

'You've been reading left-wing literature.'

Professor Rivers boomed. 'I recommend a healthy diet, a Jane Austen, and another tutorial.'

Despite myself, I laughed.

The next evening I felt much stronger.

25

I hung behind as the rest of the class filed out.

'Aha, Ruby!' He was carrying a stack of papers. Peering at me through his glasses. Sir Hugo is the kind of person who is described as 'larger than life.' And I suppose he did cultivate a certain image. For instance he preferred a three-piece suit. That evening's suit was of green corduroy, with leather patches on the elbows. I noticed his strong physique. Curly greying black hair flew around an interesting face. His blue eyes were sharp, humorous, penetrating. His gaze could flatter or intimidate.

He had a reputation in the right wing and left wing press as 'controversial'. His columns in the *Deliverer* delighted in exposing what he saw as contradictions in the lobby positions he lampooned. The 'anti-fur' lobby that exempted leather; the decline of drawing in art schools. His articles lamented loss of 'identity' he argued was accentuated by current policies.

But in the flesh, he was disconcertingly benign, strangely an attractive figure despite his stomach.

'Feeling better?' He boomed, twinkling at me.

'Yes, thank-you,' I tossed my hair back over my shoulders. This English toff better not ask me any personal questions.

'Would you care to join me for a drink?' he asked. 'I'm on my way to the Black Gizzard.'

'Okay, I'll go. For a drink,' I said staring straight back into his blue eyes.

I might have been succumbing to his confusing charm but I was determined not to let his obnoxious politics intimidate me.

As we walked, he pushing his bicycle, I was on the defensive, preparing to fall into argument. But Hugo did not seem too interested in talking politics. I brought up university cuts, the abolition of student's rent assistance. He laughed amiably, changing the subject to Plato's theory of Beauty.

'Of course Plato held,' he paused, sucking on his fag, looking at me appraisingly, 'that Beauty is the property of objects measurable in regards to purity, harmony, integrity, and perfection...hmmm?'

He raised his left eye-brow. Staring at me meaningfully.

He drank whisky; bought two glasses of burgundy for me and we arranged a time for a re-scheduled tutorial in two days time, at his house in Primrose Hill.

Day Five

Hugo

Days before we leave and I break my arm. Fell off the bike as I negotiated traffic in Gower Street. Doctor in a hurry opened his car door and—thwack! I find myself, beached and gasping on the tarmac, glad for once of the crash helmet Ruby insists I wear. I knocked my head. I'm all right apart from the arm. The bike has a badly dented front wheel that needs repair. My assailant took me to Casualty and patched me up himself.

Ruby drove me this morning in my old red coupé.

'I've just read an article that said that this car that I was given in the sixties when I was eighteen, is considered a status symbol amongst gangster drug-dealers!' I was trying to make light of it.

She smiled, then coughed, rubbing her nose. How I love to see her driving. Her strong young hands, with long purple talons, competently spinning the wheel. Pulling the handbrake with natural authority. I'd let her drive me anywhere, anytime, arm broken or not.

Luckily the left arm so not impossible 'though dashed awkward trying to pick up books and papers. Teaching is over for the break. I'm in my office working on the Ethics of Desire. Have to keep on calling Elena to help me transport leaning towers of literature from the floor and bookshelves, on all

28

kinds of fascinating subjects.

Masochism, lesbianism, homosexuality and fetishes...

Depositing them upon the desk. Ticky looks on quizzically with eyebrow raised.

Right in the middle of penultimate chapter Perversions, and it looks like it's shaping up to be my masterwork, a common sense, empirical, very English, contribution responding to the philosophy of sexuality by eighteenth and nineteenth century noblemen, which for far too long has been commandeered by the continentals. I'm pleased with research for the book (and my assistant). Elena's rather an attractive woman. Young, dark haired, Greek, good secretary though a little too timid. She hands me Sade's *One Hundred and Twenty Days of Sodom* and bolts from the room.

Must say, this cycling incident makes me wonder not for the first time if it's wise to cycle. I'd stopped cycling to work but Ruby encouraged me as she says it is necessary to keep fit.

In the beginning, I used to drive her to the gallery—it's only five minutes to Prince's. Then she became smitten with a fitness urge; that is, an urge for my fitness. But it's worth it, if it makes her happy. And it does that, only last week she complimented me on my toned thighs and calves. 'I'm sure your stomach's shrinking!' she said. I'm not at all sure I agree. 'The idea of seeing my toes when I'm standing seems remote as Zeno's arrow ever hitting its target...' I protest. But I'll take her word for it.

The slimmer, more youthful, my physique for the famed Aussie beach, the better, though the last thing I really want to do is lie around on a beach in Sydney basting like a beefsteak on a barbecue grill. But I don't want to let Ruby down. She's reserved when it comes to her feelings. And that's one of the reasons I love her.

She's far too polite, considerate, to express her desires first, epitome of a lady.

She hasn't mentioned it.

She doesn't have to. I've let her know I know what she wants. I'll be her pink skinned beach boy. Her ageing, still game Adonis, do the Ernest Hemingway in Panama hat and white flannels (surprise from my tailor hidden in my suitcase with a chiffon floral dress. And another surprise for her). I'm more than ready to dress the part, gentleman of the colonies and escort my wife around Sydney town. Better get over there quick, I've been encouraging her, while it's still linked to Britain, our beleaguered yet still gracious Queen.

I've been reading on Australian art to give her some useful tips, between the requirements of my heavy schedule, writing for *The Daily Deliverer* and *The Accord,* working away on the Ethics of Desire. My time is valuable but it's worth it to help her. I'm already giving advice on what to look for.

'You have to be careful, Ruby. Investing your, or should I say, *our* valuable time and money.'

She's been quiet, pale and distant lately. I put it down to the excitement of our impending trip, if not the art she's been showing. As soon as we get to Australia the stresses of preparing for the trip will be over. We'll be able to relax and have that long awaited holiday I keep re-assuring her. Although she endearingly insists the trip is just business I say there's no reason why that should take longer than the first three days—after all, she will have me to help her—then we've got the rest of the time to Enjoy! Enjoy! Enjoy!

It's what life is for, Ruby, I'll tell her. I'll make sure we take her sweetly conscientious mind off work. I've been waiting to meet her family, find out her tantalizing mystery for so long, everything about my wife fascinates me.

And Christmas on a beach, arm still in this damn sling, what material for a column that will be.

Ruby

Sprouts Organic Restaurant, Hale Hall, WC1

'I don't think of Australia as 'home,' Hugo,' I tell him again at lunch. 'Home is in London, Rivers Chase in Primrose Hill, the Gallery. It's here...'

I look around the restaurant with what I intend to be a bright optimistic smile.

'I don't have strong memories of Australia. I can hardly remember anything about it...vague things but they don't make any sense.'

He squints at me quizzically over a forkful of black bean and tofu pie. It's a conversation we've had numerous times in various forms.

'But if your family is there, surely Ruby you must remember something!' His voice warm with fond indulgence. I play along with the game and smile.

'I have a new family now, darling. You are my family.'

'Of course you do.' He pats my knee under the table.

'Yes, my family.'

Married to Hugo, I'm part of a family net, a close web of ties: evenings with my brother-in-law Perry, and Yvonne. Occasional tennis with my sister-in-law Harriet, phone calls with mother-in-law Demeter from the family seat in Sussex. (Not to mention Ticky, Milo, and Claris, of course).

Hugo is pleased we're going.

31

'It will be splendid to be in the South,' he says. 'What a shame you don't remember, Ruby.' He teases. 'I am so much looking forward to meeting your family,' he leans back expansively. 'Sure they are in Australia, not the old sub-continent? If they were we could visit Cousin Coddington and go mountain climbing, Everest...' he continues his bantering tone, as if it's an invitation for me to give another story.

'Mount Everest!' I snort laughter. 'That would be nice!'

Using his unslung arm he wipes his mouth with a paper serviette. Behind him, I spy a dark-haired young man in an army surplus store coat. He was in the gallery last month; he asked me if we took new work. He had been wearing a red bandana, eighteenth century brocade jacket and jodhpurs. I said come back with your portfolio, show me. Try me. I turned my attention back to Hugo.

'We're only going to be in Sydney three weeks. It's hardly enough time to even line up deals with the artists I'm interested in.'

'Come, come! Ruby, we've got to take your mind off work. You're not telling me we're going all that way without taking in some sights of your fascinating homeland. And that means doing some shopping, too!' He twinkled.

As if he thinks, by definition, women love to shop, and he, as always, is more than happy to indulge me. Shopping is an occupation that I've never had the cruelty to tell Hugo I find boring. Altogether too much is at stake. Shopping represents what has become practically a psychic bond between us. You could say it's the domestic motor of our marriage, a driver of progress and motion, there's always something more we need to buy, something we need or want.

'I'm not coming home without a Dry-your-Bones raincoat,' he smiles with a triumphant gleam in his blue eyes.

Hugo has been on his own, to an international conference on Ethics of Aesthetics. He enjoyed the food, wine, the sun, his ferry ride across Sydney Harbour, he says with a twinkle and smile, teasing, humouring me. At least I think he is. The older I am, the more blurred outlines of people appear. Who is deeply whom they seem? What life's taught me is not to trust anyone. Keep yourself hidden and you can be with anyone; do anything if you've got enough bottle, they say here. London has given me bottle galore. Maybe I need glasses.

I go to the Ladies. Lock myself in a cubicle; fish the sachet, blade, mirror from out of my Kernel bag. Shake out white crystals, chop-chop a line, snort it through a rolled-up fiver. The hit is sublime, divine, carries me to cloud nine. As I lean against the wall I see a vision, Hugo on the beach, Hugo in trunks with me in pink 1950s-style bikini, it seems hysterically funny. And what is funnier is what he will never know, what I can never tell him about life in Australia. I don't know myself.

Sniffing, smiling unable to stop, I sway my way back to the table.

Hugo looks up at me with a big smile.

'Alright, sugar?' That sets me off laughing again.

I'm Hugo's white-sugar, sugar-white girl cube, sweetness of existence essence, charging white horses, white angels through red-hot veins.

In the fairy-tale a Snow Queen kissed Kay and he forgot his name, age, and family. With a shard of ice in his heart, he forgot himself, he forgot Gerda his friend who loved him, whom he loved. He climbed into Queen's sleigh. She covered Kay with her ermine mantle. The deadly cold-hearted queen sped Kay without delay to her palace in the icy wastes where he was forced to be her slave in misery. One day Gerda, grown up, who had travelled through forests and across countries to find him, had not forgotten him, rescued him and warmed him back to life with her love.

They returned to the village where they married and lived happily ever after.

'I'm fine,' I pronounce the words with difficulty.

'I wish there were music here to drown out the sounds of cutlery, the savage implements of the feeding ritual.'

He smiles, and starts to hum *Men of Harlech*.

I push my plate aside, watching the beautiful waitresses who may one day be famous actresses, gliding around the tables as if on blades, carrying their trays as if they're on stage.

As we are leaving, I nearly fall over the feet of the artist in the greatcoat. Hugo catches me, helps me, practically carrying me through the door. Like he carried me over the threshold of Rivers Chase after the wedding.

Hugo used to ask me about growing up in Australia. He's given up. I couldn't, never think about it myself. Can't think about it, life there. It was difficult when we first met. It wasn't long after I came around. Two years. I still couldn't bear hearing the word 'Australia' mentioned, and that wasn't easy in a culture which screens Australian television shows twice or more every twenty-four hours.

When we first started going out, for drinks, then meals, then more together, the biggest social hurdle I had to negotiate with him was not living in a Regent's Park squat, being broke, and by his standards under-educated, 'Australian'.

It was that I didn't talk about my past. Couldn't talk about

34

it, about anything that had happened. Before coming around in London. I couldn't talk about Australia.

I didn't want to have to lie, to recreate a life. I was trying to forget. And I didn't want to tell him what I did remember, and the fugue. So instead of making it all up, I told him a white lie about The Accident—myself, I whispered silently to him in my fast and breathless talking.

'I was in an accident after I arrived in London.' We were in Hugo's drawing room. It was the first time he'd invited me in for drinks, we'd been to the Theatre Royale. Sipping port in front of a big black marble fireplace.

Hugo was absent-mindedly stroking the old fur coat that I used to have; I found that odd, but endearing.

'I'd just got into a taxi, it pulled out from the curb, I didn't have time to fasten my seat belt. Suddenly the taxi swerved to miss a cyclist, it ran into a Stop sign, my head hit the window, I was in hospital for weeks. I lost all memory of my past life and myself.

For a whole week I had no recollection whatsoever of who I was. Then islets of memory began to emerge from oblivion… name, age, date of birth, facts. There's still a huge amount I am sure I don't remember, distressing to try, it comes back by itself, it can be upsetting…'

I gazed into dancing flames. Hugo was so sympathetic, I almost felt guilty. My survival mechanism empowered me to push it away.

His hands moved from stroking my fur coat to stroking my hair. He took me upstairs into his bedroom, he made love with tenderness, intelligence, and I forgot his age, which in normal circumstances, that is if Hugo was not Hugo and I was myself, I don't imagine I would have done. But after that night, romance blossomed. There was nothing he wouldn't do.

And with Hugo, for once I felt safe, secure, looked after.

I didn't need to think about Australia.

And for what seemed a long time but was only months, a year, the Past left me alone. I was free and happy in my new life. Living in the present.

It wasn't until I'd moved into Rivers Chase, not until my new life was underway, that dreams and intrusive memories, began to haunt and torment me with all the power of a guilty secret. Like the hidden history of a photograph.

A worm eating into the heart of a delectable piece of fruit, a juicy mango, whose sweetness it will contaminate, poison.

The haunting bars of fugue drift through the air. A young woman violinist is playing in the fading light of a big room. Illuminated by a sunbeam. Hovering in darkness I can almost see a phantom-beauty. Heart-shaped face, crimson lips, dark eyes, black hair, arms, flickering fingers, vibrating strings. A slight figure dressed in black gilded by the dying sun. Her face transfigured by passion, yet her bow commands release of exquisite expression as if she is on the brink of an ecstatic revelation. A vision.

Untitled #1

Untitled #2

Hugo

Princes University College, Friday afternoon

Death of the Author. The mid-twentieth-century critical studies movement had profound impact in Australia where its main tenet was known literally as 'death of the author.' In the essay by Barthes his insight was to point out that in the process of writing, the author-God disappears into their text. To what extent are the words one writes one's own? To what extent is one responsible for what one writes? To what extent could a text in which an author disappears, reveal the disappearance?

Listen to this I said last night to Ruby in bed, from *Venus in Furs* by our friend Leopold von Sacher-Masoch.

Ruby

Ruby Gallery

I saw his gigantic hand plunging down into a jar, scooping me out and popping me into his mouth. When I awoke lying next to him in bed, it seemed like I was still in a pickling bottle. As if I'd met my inner self in my dream.

Now I'm at my desk. But in my pickling bottle, my bell jar, frozen as I am, I dream. I long for more. I long for a way out, an exit into bliss.

And, if last night's dream was bad, it was, in a way, a relief. Maybe even a development. Dreaming I was pickled in a jar, at least I was not having one of the dreams that haunt me.

How many. Couldn't count. Wouldn't want to. Don't think about dreams. Haven't. Pushed them away. Back down into the slime. Monsters. The darkest, secret reaches of my mind.

Raymond.

Did anyone hear me? The gallery is quiet. It's raining in the Walk. Presumably in the next street and street after that. Presumably it's raining in all the streets of London. Rain in the city and you could be anywhere. Rain, a soft blurring merge of line, colour, and form. Holding together all the streets of a crying city, crying mind. Did I speak out loud? My God, got to get a grip. Pull up socks. Tuck in shirt-tails. Adjust skirt. Walk into the store-room and smoke a cigarette, pacing up and down, up, until I can't stand it, the pressure in my head, I clutch for mirror, plastic sachet, in my Kernel clutch bag. White sugar-crystals of my delight. Shake it out, chop-chop-

39

chop, roll a fiver, carefully, snort a quick ecstatic line.

Our experiences have been committed to eternity
Nothing can touch our past.

Lines by Raymond. A letter he wrote long ago.

Untitled #3

You confuse me but I love it. Our experiences have been committed to experience. You commit me but I experience it. Our commitments have been experienced to Eternity. You love it but I confuse me. Our love has been experienced to Eternity, you confuse it but

Back at my desk I open a manilla file folder. Aboriginal art. A sculptural series, the word RAPED spelt in used bullets set in smoked steel. The 3-D word ADDICTED constructed in bullets. 3-D word-sculpture SUGAR made from solidified shiny white crystals, sprinkled with blood. I read:

Handouts to Aboriginal farm workers, of sugar, tea, and opium had the effect of fettering them with addictions. Those seen as 'recalcitrant' were especially at risk of sugar and flour rations laced with arsenic.

Images. A tea setting with a sugar-bowl on a lace skull, a silver skull-topped spoon, a bowl of sugar, the bowl is made of china with patterns depicting scenes of Aboriginal people shackled by neck and leg irons. A bowl depicting scenes of Aboriginal people hanging in trees. Another shows scenes of the rape of Aboriginal women, the word 'SHAME' covering their bodies; another: Aboriginal children taken by authorities with the word 'STOLEN' in copperplate script.

I read that White Sugar is by a woman artist, Buradyara and is her personal response to finding 'hidden history' of her family discovered in research in Queensland state archives, oral records. I read that sugar was laced with arsenic, given to Aboriginal workers on station farms in the time when the Aboriginal people were being moved off their land.[8]

This work is of a hidden history, and is as much history as art. The work is about the untold numbers of Aboriginal

41

people shackled by addiction, and killed. Made from the perspective of Aboriginal descendants. A set of teacups in which rest child-size black skulls, reminiscent of nightmarish eggs in eggcups.

WHITE SUGAR made from white crystals and blood. White cubes of sugar.

So that you can drink your tea sweet, sugar.

I hear words tracking through my mind, a woman's voice, tinkling of teacups on saucers. A vision of a grandmother, an image of a fireplace, two arms reaching out from it, the black iron surround, as if a woman is imprisoned behind. I see an elegant hand spooning sugar ladling it into a bone-china teacup.

Day Three

Ruby

Sunday morning

Dream Rays
Last night I
Dreamed of him again
The same as all the dreams
The same but different
Although each plays out a
Different scene the form is
The same
I've got a
A dream
Template stuck in my brain

Boiling eggs through a hungover haze. My left nostril feels burnt; nauseous. Doing my best to look intelligent and competent, qualities that seem impossibly desirable required attributes in this situation I feel more out of than in.

'December is a splendid time,' Hugo is saying from his seat at the breakfast table as he pours Earl Grey from the pot onto the milk in his teacup.

Hugo is fastidiously particular when it comes to routines such as the 'right' way to drink tea.

'Christmas!' He ladles spoons of sugar, stirring vigorously. Why worry about order of pouring milk and tea and leaves over bags only to kill the flavour with sweetness? One of his idiosyncrasies that privately crack me up.

'I'll happily exchange this darkness and gloom,' he takes a noisy sip from his cup and peers through the kitchen window into the shady terrace garden as if having trouble with his vision, 'for the Sun! Those Beaches!'

Like many people I have met in England, Hugo seems to share a fetish for warm climates, illogical as some people's predilection for shopping malls. As if just because the sky is blue and sun shining, or the shops covered by one roof things are really going to be any different in your life.

I smile, as I lift eggs from the boiling water and put them on Yoon's kitten tea towel on the bench top.

'We'll be back for New Year in the country with Mother, but I hope that we will be able to see your family and wish them a Happy Christmas this year, too!' Hugo is surely being ironical but he seems genuinely pleased by this.

I almost feel guilt for being uninvolved. I've been trying to think of the right way to let Hugo know. He wants me to have a family. I'll try to find a way to tell him when we arrive. We do not get on. I was kicked out. She took my place. I have not contacted them, nor tried to.

As I smash the top of my boiled egg, images from a dream come back at me in a swirling rush.

Hurrying downhill towards the jetty with a large wooden structure on it. The sky is clear blue. Grass is green. The jetty structure is dark and solid. He is in there. An object of desire, of gravity towards which I can't stop myself from falling, fast.

In the beginning, I am always on my way to meet him.

I am running, drawing nearer, trying to give an illusion of cool. All I think of is he. Now I am inside the structure I see him. Red hair. He is alone, absorbed in his work masterpiece.

I always find him alone absorbed in work. I walk up quietly and he looks up; it is, as it always seems to be, in the deepest sense. Of being joined. Part of something bigger than I. He talks to me (often in the dream series our bond is silent). He talks about writing, I talk about my writing and as we do, it is as if we somehow become a part of writing; and doing the writing at the same time, in my secret inner dream narrative. It's the deepest I've ever felt for anyone; and as the moment settles around us in its intense power, it is broken.

The moment of perfection, a crystal prism, shatters. She comes running towards us, bursts into our private rendezvous. The tone of her voice, imperious. Automatically, he switches into her realm of focus. Quick as a dog responding to its mistress's call. And I? I shrink. Shrink. Shrivel, and shrink—until I disappear.

Untitled #4

In how-many days, I can't work out exactly how many due to the time difference my mind can't grasp that we are really going, I will be in that landscape of beauty and terror...Words echo in my head, phantoms disconnected from thoughts, my feelings. Staring at my egg as if I've just seen a human foetus curled up there. I feel sick. I'm aware of Hugo's eyes as I stand up suddenly, hurriedly, and rush to the downstairs bathroom. I only just have time to make it before retching violently.

Vomiting, bringing up bile over the toilet, head spinning.

And Hugo is right behind me asking if I'm all right. He is assisting me to the drawing room, helping me onto the otto-man couch. His hand is on my feverish brow taking my pulse, his voice is saying I mustn't go to the Gallery today. Rest, I must rest. Need to rest.

Hugo

We wanted to have a special evening for you and Ruby before you go!' Yvonne giggled and fluttered her eyelashes flirtatiously. Really. As if we were going to the Other Side of the world for two years rather than two weeks... But I must say despite convenience of modern travel there is something ineffably distant about Australia.

I'm excited about the prospect of being there. Just knowing it's as far as one can travel from England is quite thrilling. (Although I am doing this for Ruby in my unceasing attempt to help her find her lost family).

For myself, I consider Philosophy to be the most meaningful travel adventure.

But it is essential to have contrast as Aristotle observed: the Good Man, and of course Good Woman, need balance to thrive. Holiday, an adventure, every now and then, is just the remedy...

Talking of adventures, look at our history of colonizing the continent. Only two hundred and forty years ago it didn't exist, at least not as we know it now. James Cook, the cartographer turned ship's captain set off in the little ship of wood and iron the Endeavour, wind cracking the sails, set off to sail across the world, to find the 'Great Southern Land' that was long believed must exist to balance northern continents. The Enlightenment had inspired art and culture opening to ideas of infinity, an endlessly expanding world... Flat-earthers believed the captain fell off the edge when his ship disappeared over the horizon, but he sailed on. Cook's instruction was to sail to Tahiti to chart the astronomical Transit of Venus.

After that, he opened a sealed document from the King, with instructions to sail on and find the continent that had been written of from Aristotle onward. After more months of sailing, hopes of success, fears of failure, they found the shore England longed to find. Aboriginal people had long settled the land. England staked a claim based on a wrong presumption of terra nullius as they did not live in recognisable cities or towns, and soon England was exporting 'undesirables' the rowdy poor filling up slums and city streets, petty criminals, 'Rebels' from Ireland in the colonial uprisings of 1797 and 1803, political exiles, banished to the new world.

'Cook landed at an inlet he at first called Sting Ray Bay and changed to Botany Bay, which became the basis of the penal colony.'

Ruby blanched. I thought she may have swallowed a fish bone—in Yvonne's chowder. 'Are you alright, Ruby?' Yvonne had noticed her state as well.

Ruby took a time to answer. Her eyes glazed, and distant, face drained of blood. I was about to slap her back to loosen the bone, but suddenly she appeared to come around with a jolt as if waking up or coming out of a trance state. She shook her head, blinked her eyes, and looked confused.

'Yes, I'm fine, I just remembered something.' She shouted.

As if calling to me in my study. The entire table was looking at her in alarmed anticipation, waiting for Ruby to finish. She said nothing then she laughed abruptly, suddenly oddly bright.

'I forgot some materials from the Gallery some catalogues I need for our trip, I'll have to pick them up—you don't mind, do you, Hugo?' She smiled sweetly over the cranberry sauce at me, would have brought a frozen cadaver to life. That was Ruby. Always worrying about with art business matters.

'Not still thinking about work?' I rebuked her. 'Can't you relax for this evening? Forget the gallery. Relax. Relax! Enjoy! Company! Food! Conversation! Chowder!! Of course I'll go, in a cab, pick up your things later...Come, drink, and forget. Allow me to propose the toast. To Australia, Land of Hope and Promise!!'

'To Australia!' Their voices echoed mine and I was pleased to observe Ruby's fleeting smile, flitting like a shadow across her features as she raised a glass to her crimson lips and drank.

Ruby

In the middle of the soup it came back to me. Was it imagination playing tricks; was it fantasy or—a memory? I was in the bush. At the top of the small mountain. I'd climbed up, to be alone. Margy had set off for the banks of the creek. She was going to the Platypus Pool to try to find some cool air in the willows' shade, she'd said. Wearing the beekeeper hat as sunhat, and her black silk slip, emerald green silk blouse, bright orange bag with water bottle and book, slung over her shoulder.

Ray had departed to go sketching before I'd left the house. I didn't know where he planned to go. It was afternoon. The land was slipping and sliding in a haze, forty-three degrees Celsius.

Buzzing, shrieking cicadas. I climbed up the track, which we cleared years before. Up the steep side of Mount Capricorn rising behind the wooden farmhouse. Onto the plateau at the edge of which was a red flat-topped boulder above a rocky precipice.

As I headed to the rock, I passed a snake in the white-gold crunchy grass. A brown, fully grown, at least two metres long. Their venom could be lethal. But I wasn't worried. I was used to seeing snakes. Brown, black, red-belly blacks, three of the deadliest writhed over the land in the foothills of the mountains. The country was a snakes' paradise. I always saw one when I walked alone. I abided by clothing rules: wore boots and socks, and I carried a snake-stick, snapped off from fallen boughs. If you tapped the ground ahead, it alerted snakes. The king brown slithered away. I reached my rock.

Lay down on its warm surface. Gazed east into the shimmering canyons of light, drifting mauve horizon, land I secretly termed Paradise Plains.

That's when I saw them.
Two tiny figures, flagrant emerald next to black,
Walking together by the creek.
A couple of k's from me.[9]
Margy and Ray, walking together.
They must have met up, I recall thinking.
I thought nothing of it.
Why should I have?
I was pleased to see them—wherever they were.
After everything that had happened in the family.
My best friend and my lover.
The two people I loved most intensely
The image so vivid I was stunned
I disappeared

I wasn't sure where I was, lost, displaced

A moment of unreality
Then Hugo' s face swam towards me

And I snapped back
Hugo' s booming voice
Pulling me into
The world
back
into
focus

Like wandering into another country, reflective self-based writing derived from traumatic experience involving a sense of alienation and dissociation is a form of metaphorical inner journey that provides a release, albeit painful, perhaps, which a writer cannot find anywhere else, or in any other way, in the culture in which they live.

Day Two

Margarita

16, The Mayfair, George Street, Sydney

Something strange keeps happening. It started at around the time the jacaranda tree outside the window of my office burst into vivid purple blossom. At about the time summer's scorching promise (white light, heat, hallucinogenic intensity) slid slyly then violently into the days that had been fresh, contained by spring. It started with a realization that I often think of as a threat, of impending summer.

A high-pitched shrieking... Relentless, incongruous, and the sudden silence when it stops is equally shocking. But it doesn't stop, it only pauses for a minute or two then resumes its solitary screeching with ferocious gusto.

A cicada, harbinger of summer, has hi-jacked its way into my apartment. And I can't get the sound out.

Every evening as the sky empties before nightfall it starts. Shrieking. I don't know where it's coming from, how it's surviving, here in the centre of the city. The nearest greenery is a dusty-leaved plane tree on the side of the street. I don't have a plant. Every evening I try to locate the insistent insect. Pace the large loft apartment. Open the glass doors that lead onto the narrow balcony. I lean on the railing. The thunder of peak hour traffic on the street below conceals all other noise. I look everywhere. In stainless cupboard drawers of the open-plan kitchen. The bathroom. Under rugs. I've found cockroaches (even here, in this building), but no cicada.

I stand in the centre of the living room trying to pinpoint exactly where it's coming from. But every time I start to walk towards where I think it is, it switches.

Yesterday I told Ray and he cackled harshly. 'You're hearing things you've been alone in the deathstyle apartment too long. Come back and live with me... Come back to. Alchemy Studios.'

I heard anger in his voice.

I looked around the kitchen where we were drinking tea. Peeling paint. Asbestos walls. Ants swarming in trails of spilt sugar. I smiled, and shook my head. It has taken all my new confidence to achieve independence, break free from Ray and all that held me to him.

Now is the first time I do not need someone else with a desperation that had enslaved me.

'I think I can live with a cicada exile, Ray,' I laughed.' It's not exactly *Eraserhead*.' We had seen the film at the Valhalla.

He laughed. 'Maybe it's just the start,' he said. 'Watch out for men with flat-tops.'

I smiled, looked away. I didn't want to shag him; I shouldn't go there anymore. Sometimes he asks, bluntly: 'Why are you here, charity visit, is it?'

But he's the person I feel closest to.

Despite Rosamond, and all that happened, maybe because of it, he's my best friend. Or that's what I like to think.

Battling cicadas, I try another tactic. Drowning the sound by playing CDs of Chopin. Beethoven. Bach. My recording. The unfinished fugue, *Contrapunctus 14*, a fragment.

I undress alone, unwatched, unacknowledged, except perhaps by cicada. Slip into my purple nightshirt and prepare for bed. Slide under a sheet; it's too hot for a duvet.

At night beyond the pool of peach-coloured-light cast by my lamp, dark shadows stripe the floor; I am reminded, chillingly, of the apartment in Adelaide, that Roz and Ray found. The nights in the bed where they had lain together. Watching eerie shadows strobe the walls as the broken street-light flickered and hissed outside...

Screeching, vertigo of consciousness, and again
the brilliant glitter, cicada-shriek of
the Farm in summer.

The Farm. Winter evenings sitting before the wood fire, eating stew, playing games. In the summertime, we gathered on the veranda in armchairs inherited from Roz's grandparents, whiling away moonlit nights, playing violin and flute, with a chorus of cicadas, delicious fragrance of earth floating under a sky of bright stars that looked as if it went on forever.

It may feel as if I hadn't been to The Farm since Roz left, but that's not quite accurate, I did go, once. But it didn't seem to count. I'd rung Aphrodite. She was delighted to hear my voice, she said. Invited me to dinner, I hadn't seen her for over a year.

She didn't mind about Ray, he was welcome she said. He was surprised, cynically. But that was his state of mind. Still, I remembered, Aphrodite's reception when he had visited Roz in her Mother's terrace house in Glebe years before, had been less than friendly.

I think she was glad to see I had a boyfriend now.

Especially since Rosamond disappeared.

Aphrodite was effusive with concern. In her smart suit, hair styled, Roz's mother appeared elegant as ever.

'You must be lonely. You were going to go there together, weren't you?'

I smiled. 'I'm fine Aphrodite, don't worry about me.'

But it wasn't as it used to be going down to The Farm the last time. Aphrodite drove Raymond and myself there. She said she'd like to have a look at the old place again. We went for the afternoon.

The grass around the farmhouse was bleached white gold. The man who lived up the road hadn't been running horses on the land. I was terrified of snakes hidden from sight in the long dry grass.

The key was still on the ledge above the door. I opened the padlocked door to Roz's old room off the end of the veranda. Trod softly into waiting darkness. Pulled back the curtain and peered through yellow and purple panes in colonial windows that Wolfie had found near the river, carried back, and installed for her. Through bumpy yellow glass whorls pale green willow trees looked sickly and insipid. I felt suddenly queasy.

I lay on the big colonial bed that was made up as if she was just about to return any time. The bed I had slept in before her days of de facto Wolfie. When it was freezing cold in winter, and we shared the bed to share the bedding, trying to kindle body-heat under layers of blankets, towels, rugs, coats, all the material fabrics we could find to pile on until the covers were so heavy we couldn't move, and we were still frozen in her bed.

Now it was heat that suffocated, pounding my temples.

Shrieking cicadas seemed lodged in my brain, a crescendo rising inside my ears. I didn't have time to stand. I vomited all over the eau-de-nil bed cover heirloom from her grandmother.

Raymond

Margo moved the manikins, part of my new piece, which were dangling suspended from the ceiling into our bedroom, in deference to the old stick. As we were about to leave had a king-hit of smack in the bedroom, just me in there with mannequins and spoon—HA! That got me down there pleasantly numb and detached, for the first part of the trip, then, scratching, restless, bones aching. Marg gabbling to the old stick, trying to deflect attention from my despicable state tsk! Junkie-Ray in his gutter, ripping skin from his flesh with his nails, not exactly the ideal escort for 'the girls'. I'd brought smoking smack, not the best hit but gets you through times of crisis, just made it to toilets at the gas station where we stopped—whoosh! Got my hit on the dunny.

And language, feeling, and every need that drives you mad ceased. Nodding out, like a fuzzy wobble-headed dog people used to put in the rear windows of cars so when you'd be driving along you'd be staring at a toy St Bernard or poodle head wibbling and swinging away. That was Boy-Ray crouched in Rosa's Ma's car, shivering idiot-toy-dog nodding, wobbling feebly as the children in the car behind screeched with joy to see wobbly dog's antics. And I was one of those happy-happy children setting off on a happy-happy holiday...

Stumbled along behind Mara-ta who despite my blighted presence was still babbling away in a convincing impression of a Normal Person to Rosa's Ma who did not seem to have noticed that World War Three had broken out behind her guest's eyes the stick wasn't paying any attention to him at all and I was desperate, had to get it, had to get out of it, had to get a fix before the eyes exploded.

All I had was pissy smoking smack.

Smoked a joint in Rosa's old room. The smell made Marge throw up on the sickly striped rug. Or maybe it was the sight of me, hideous vision of wasted youth, dreams—O horror— her nemesis, sprawled out on the cold and empty bed of our long-lost dear departed one. HA!

'Take a little toke; it'll perk you up, make you feel a million bucks. Make you forget Rosa, the whole goddamn.' I held out the joint to her. 'For god's sake,' she said in that snooty voice. 'Can't you do without it for one afternoon? Can't you at least make an effort?'

Well no, Marga, that's what being a junkie means. That's when she strewth! Projectile technicolour yawn all over the rug.

Heavens, what would our dear departed one have thought?

Ruby

Order
Control
Organize file tidy
Dominate
Get on top

My nails clipped short, every single hair painstakingly removed by Miss Pauline in waxing and exfoliation at The Beauty Spot, Covent Garden. I want nothing to grow out of my skin. I want to stay below surface. Cast the slightest neatest shadow. Keep inside any tendency to natural growth. Clip it back; rip it out at root. Present artificial face, my alabaster-pale smooth skin. My perfect mask.

Hugo likes me in a mask. Feathers, velvet, sparkles, studs, leather, gas mask. He puts his hands to my face and runs his fingers blindly over the strange braille of desire. What Hugo sees or feels, Hugo gets, which is a disguise.

I am waiting for him to decide which one to take. Will it be one of the masks that have become me? From the costume box.

Black velvet eye-mask, peaks above eye-spaces edged with silver sequins. The masked ball classic.

Cats-eye. Tawny tabby furry stripes.

Tyger Tyger, burning bright/ In the forests of the night;/ What immortal hand or eye [10]

In a cats-eye mask I am Cat. Lion, tiger, panther, puma, feline huntress racing over Savannah muscles rippling intent on one thing only: nailing its quarry.

This is the script he has written for me to perform. I have to jump on his back, rip and claw skin with long talons, and teeth, or pretend to, until he rolls over purring.

Every night for three years our bedroom has evoked the scene of his fantasy. Peacock feathers, masks, whips, and furs. A velvet opera gown. All the finery and accessories of the 'Ideal Woman', Boadicea, Cleopatra, Josephina, Venus in furs, he scripts me to play. Theatre and ritual have taken over our life.

I must conclude that, my husband, already older than me, is older in his taste, he would have been better suited to living in the nineteenth century fin de siècle.

It's been like this since he started research for the book he is writing on the Ethics of Desire.

He says he is now a phenomenologist and it is essential for the phenomenologist to work through experience, to reach the thing-in-itself, find truth after casting of or 'bracketing' so far as possible, social conditioning, preconceived thoughts and ideas.

I have been his assistant.

How did it get to this? Three years ago, when I was looking for him and he was not in his study in the attic, I found a draft advertisement Hugo had written. On his desk.

Wanted. Adventurous broad-minded women to play parts in theatrical tableaux for research project into the psychology of Leopold von Sacher-Masoch's nineteenth century representations of desire.

I confronted him with it, and said to him that I did not want him to be involved in research projects with assistants, other women. I said I would play these archaic parts. At first, he seemed put out that I had found his advertisement, said that he was not going to publish it, he had made it up, it was fiction, and research in itself. And then, somewhat to my surprise, he said how surprised, shocked, he was I should suggest this, as I was his wife.

I couldn't trust him when he said that he would not publish the advertisement, and find a young research assistant, or maybe two or three, who knew where it could all lead. After a week of concerted persuasion he agreed. But he said that if we were to do this, we had to do it by way of a contract, this was a part of it, in the literature. It was like acting in a play. I agreed. So now we have three different contracts, we are partners in my Gallery, and it is separate to our marriage contract.

It was precisely because of our marriage, my desire to keep it that I suggested this though I did not say that to Hugo, and for a long time I was suspicious of his assurances that he was not going to place that advertisement, or another like it.

I did not want to share —or lose—my husband to a Ph.D.

candidate freelancing in sexual psychoanalytical research who might try to seduce him with stunningly original feminist theories of fetishism, disavowal, suspense, interpretations of 'three mothers' and capitalism as she trampled Hugo's back in furs and other props he would doubtless supply. And I knew they were out there.

I worried when I found his advertisement, determined to do what I could to forestall such an emergency.

At the same time I thought it was ironic. There used to be an idea that women could escape the poverty-trap through a university degree but increasingly women had to revert to the 'oldest profession' to pay off the indexed loans for education fees. Many higher degree students could not pay the loans for university even by doing that work. Luckily for me I completed my Bachelors when it was free. But I did not think that others not so fortunate should have to pay and go into this kind of servitude to pay to supposedly improve their lives through education. (Albeit it was marriage that enabled me to start-up my Gallery and have the life I had now).

Just that day I read an article in the *Advocate* on this—that quoted a brothel owner who said that in her day people went to university to avoid this kind of life but now they had this kind of life so they could afford to go to university. It was wrong that it should be thus.

The contract is in my nineteenth-century writing desk in the mistress bedroom. It was my understanding that this was to be for a more limited period than has eventuated. Still, the way it is written leaves it open, until the 'book is finished'.

Hugo adapted the contract from one by a nineteenth century professor of history he has been reading for years. I don't think he gets it or he is just slow, I want a relationship with a real expression of feeling and love and this is the epitome of artificiality, everything in code, in disguise, or dramatized to a level of high theatricality. It was fun at first, but I am tired of dramatization and his endless 'scenarios'.

'Surely you've been researching this for three years now... Isn't it almost finished? Can't you move?' I ask. He laughs his booming laugh saying with a typically wicked twinkle in his eyes, 'a little more research is needed, Ruby, there are still a few angles I'm unsure of...'

As I pack my bags, I choose clothes, costumes, with care.
I need all the help I can get.
I've seen Miss Pauline. I'm toned fit, exfoliated waxed.
All my clothes are inscribed with other's names.
Beneath a barricade of designers I am invisible.

Hugo

Rivers Chase, Tuesday, 11 December 2001

Peacocks can't fly. That's what I had always thought. They are bred to be beautiful strutting proudly over manicured lawns. I keep peacock feathers, the decorative plumage, on the wall opposite our bed. After nights when the peacock mask flew, for research purposes, I took utmost care to replace it on the hook before going to sleep. We kept the door open with a light on as Ruby is, charmingly, afraid of the dark...

In the gloom of the night-time boudoir, I can see the mask still. Sometimes I glance up at it reverently as I am going to sleep. Emerald eyes glitter all-powerfully through eye-spaces. I spaces. Her eye spaces. And her voice echoes through time, through my mind, uttering the eleventh commandment.

What do you deserve, Sir Hugo. Tell me. I can't hear you,

Hugo; you'll have to speak up, Sir Hugo.

Thou shalt find salvation beyond the edge of pain.

In small dark cloistered rooms at the back of chapel, beatings grew ever fiercer as the bells for morning-song rang out at 9:00 a.m. Under ministering hands of the Brothers, Father Montague and his paddle, many of the boys grew up angry. I grew with desire that has dominated my life, my inner realm with intoxicating images I cannot shake; that shakes me until I'm quivering like a youth again. The image of a beautiful imperious woman whose attentions are deadly. Divine. Close my eyes and feel delicious lashes cracking through time and space in the private place where she will always be my master.

We did not attend school from the start in England. We try to keep that to ourselves. Myself and the nursery chaps. Ticky, the donkey. Milo, sausage dog. And Claris bear who's lost an eye. (Who are all patiently waiting in the old nursery room until we start our family). I was sent to St Ignatius in a leafy suburb at the edge of Ottawa at the age of five when Father, Earl of Rum, was Ambassador. I joined them for holidays until we returned to England. I finished my schooling at Railton, where we all agreed I should always have been.

In the boudoir, I look at the mask on the wall. I look up at it as I fall asleep, emerald eyes shine through her-spaces, as her voice echoes through time, my mind.

She is golden eagle as she flies. Proudly, gracefully, soaring into blue skies when I was not looking, didn't see. Should have packed peacock plumage not golden eagle. Foolish. What to expect heading for that wide-open land? Why couldn't I see it. Not notice the warning signs? Strange behaviour in one who was assertive...So strong. Peacocks. They are bred to look beautiful. Happy with their lot. If we'd packed peacock feathers, maybe, just maybe, she would be here with me now.

But I found out I was wrong. Peacocks can fly.

Ruby

Rivers Chase, Tuesday night

It's the night before departure and Hugo is talking about his research topic. It's 'intellectual aspect.'

'It involves playful exploitation of power balance inherent in all relationships. If both parties enjoy the—'

He lectures.

'The contract of masochism, is symbolic of the contract at the root of capitalist society and economy, the binding terms a contract sets.'

I remain impervious. Staring into the yellow violet-edged flames in the antique Italian white marble fireplace in the book-lined Hall. Sipping port. Silence in-between our words, outside roaring trees shake their branches on the Hill.

'Trusting it is mutual fulfilment of need, that motivates the love-as-violence, violence-as-love.' He says.

'Like the economy,' I say, making a joke. He laughs.

'That's where argument and analogy fail, when you apply to capitalism in practice, leaders need to be careful they don't push privileges too far in institutions of politics place themselves above laws they prescribe. Or else the contract of laws society relies on will be broken, and there will be Revolution. It has happened,' he says.

I am swinging.

On a tall swing in a small playground, beneath the apartment building next to the beach and jetty in Adelaide. I see myself as I imagine you see me. Staring from the third-floor window, high above the beach, the jetty, bait and tackle shop. My red circular-skirted gypsy dress is blowing around me. I wear it in our performances. Margy plays violin, I dance, mimicking a wind-up doll. Leaning back, long red hair blown by the wind. Sea, sky, collide, explode in prisms of light penetrating my eyes, my mind, my heart, love—for you....

I wish Nietzsche literally was right about eternal return, and that time would come again; the return would be eternal.

I think of you standing there watching from that window.

After-words.

After the fact.

A Ray-glow lingers in neuron-cells hovering in the air of eyes-closed, mind-open not-sleep. An after-image projected into my inner body, injected into inner-mind, my secret lover, my obsession.

He walks within me. Sleeps inside me. At night as I glide into sleep, he is the one I rush to meet.

Driving me mad, impossible desire, a yearning that cannot be satisfied, memory of a longing, or longing for a memory, it's so confused, crazy; I don't know what to think. When I'm not thinking.

I'm forgetting something. But I can't think what it is.

The last thing I would do is see an analyst. If an analyst had even a hint of what's seething away inside, I wouldn't rate my chances. They'd lock me up or have me on heavy-duty psych. drugs straight away.

After the procedure, the doctor at the health centre I went to suggested I see a counsellor.

'I must let you know, the counsellor in this clinic is eight months pregnant.' I laughed darkly, aware of the eyes of the pragmatic, short-haired Scottish doctor in tan leather jacket. I knew what she must be thinking—is she cracking?

I decided not to consult anyone about my pain, which I endure. What's the point in talking about it? What difference would it make? It's my pain. I have to deal with it myself.

If Dr Mael's face contorts with barely concealed disgust if I tell about my latest and I've enough symptom twinges to fill a hefty volume: Career Woman as Paranoid Neurotic: A Case Study; if they prescribe tranquillizers for my fear of opening doors in case I freeze walking through doorways, a symptom of Parkinson's Disease, it's true I read it in a deeply disturbing book; then what would she, or the shrink she'd no doubt refer me to, do if I blurted out what really troubles me?

The difficulties of living up to a fantasy Ideal Woman.

When I started studying at the London university college I became excited by the possibilities. At last I thought I was where I belonged! In the realm of thought. Intellectual life.

But the longer I stayed, the more I learned about complex social codes and private conventions that structured his inner life, I began to wonder, how far could he think beyond and outside those?

How deeply did he love me beyond masks and disguises, the fantasies? How far would he stand by me if all the trappings fell away? Would he love me if I became permanently disfigured, or some terrible fate befell me? How real was his love for me?

'Hugo.'

'Yes?'

'According to Brentano's theory of intentionality—'

'Hmmm…' he says.

'Everything we think of exists as an object of thought in our minds right? And it's that inexistent object, idea of that thing, to which thoughts, feelings, desires are directed...'

'Hmmm...'

'So that if I am thinking of Paris, it's not a 'real' city denoted by word 'Paris' I am thinking about it's the idea comprising a conglomerate of knowledge and impressions of Paris that is an inexistent object of thought that I'm thinking about.'

'Hmm...'

'So if I were to say, I'm in love with someone, I desire them, it's not a real person I'm thinking of and desiring, it's my idea of that person, I desire.'

He is watching me with an alarmed expression on his face.

'So does it not logically follow that we can never connect with the 'objects' of our desire, we're only ever relating to our fantasies and dreams, our ideas, of or about that person?'

'Ruby, all you have done is prove the danger of trying to apply logical principals outside the realm of logical possibility, that is to real life. Language shivers to abstraction within the realm of logic. Come here!'

He pulls me onto his lap.

'The Marquis had a theory about women philosophers,' he says in a playful tone. 'Tell me if you think the aristocratic French reprobate had a valid point!' He roars with drunken laughter, but doesn't continue.

'Yes?' I have glanced at his books by Sade. I am prepared for the worst.

'Well, I'll tell you because you're intelligent enough to understand what this really means...' he fixes me with a wicked beam from his blue eyes.

'And you know what libertines in *One Hundred and Twenty Days of Sodom* did to the women philosophers, Ruby?' He pauses staring with narrowed eyes into the flickering flames.

66

'They raped them and tortured and executed them.'

'I see,' I say curtly, curling my lip. 'How charming.'

'However,' he mops his brow and is smiling apologetically at me. 'They spared gallery directors!' He pushes himself up from the velvet hollow of his favourite armchair, advancing to me with big hand outstretched.

'To the bedroom, Ruby!' Hugo bellows. 'Come, you and I, for a touch of Philosophy in the Boudoir!'

'Hugo, you must have forgotten? We need to rest. Tonight I sleep—alone—in the mistress bedroom.'

I stand up.

Turn on my heel and walk across the large airy space of the Hall.

At any point I know that I could turn around and return. But I don't. I keep on walking away.

I walk up the three flights of stairs to the mistress bedroom. Open the drawer of the ladies writing desk; take out a leather bound ledger and find our typed contract for his book research.

I smooth out the page and read.

<u>Contract between Countess Ruby Rivers and Professor Hugo Rivers</u>

On his word of honour, Professor Hugo Rivers undertakes to be the servant of Mrs Countess Ruby Rivers, and carry out her desires scripted by him for the length of the project, as research for his book, The Ethics of Desire.

On her behalf, Mrs Ruby Rivers must feel free to creatively dramatise the scenarios that he devises, and to not otherwise deviate from these.

We the undersigned hereby confirm this contract.

Professor Hugo, Lord of Rivers

Countess Ruby of Rivers

I fish out a cigarette lighter from my handbag. Set light to a corner of the contract. A flame races up the page. Drop it to the floorboards, it's burning brightly. I stamp with the soles of my black leather boots, crushing flames, until all that remains is a pile of black ashes. I sweep the ashes into a tissue, and drop it in the bin.

What is most subversive about my action is that I do not tell Professor Sir Hugo what I have done.

Transports of Rapture

Boeing 747, London-Sydney. 32,000 feet

We're finally on the way. In the plane. Hugo is snuffling beside me in sleep like a big beached creature for whom I feel a sudden rush of affection. All he's done for me, it's true…

When I compare my life with him in London to the years before Hugo it seems hard to believe. Believe it, Ruby; it's your life, fate, and destiny... It's real baby...

In the funnel of overhead light, cocoon of illumination in a sleeping plane, my stockings' metallic sheen makes me want to slide on top of Hugo and wake him with a surprise.

There's something about the moneyed hush and swish of a First Class cabin, flying at 32,000 feet at night, cutting the sky like a proverbial knife through silk. I look around. *On the night before Christmas there was quiet in the house/ not a creature was stirring, not even a mouse...*[11] No lights on, nor crew in sight.

4:37 a.m. Whatever that time means up here. Flying through hemispheres, crossing Time zones, is the ultimate transgression of natural rhythm…

Up here time means nothing, normality is subverted, at any moment we could fall spinning and burning through the sky, terrorists wrenching us from our comfort zone into terrifying nightmares…Reaching up I flick the switch, and we are hidden in darkness. I slide over into Hugo's compartment.

69

Hugo

Naughty brave Ruby. My Venus, my vixen.

Despite the curtains around our cubicles, I suspected from the knowing look of the lissom air hostess—serving matching trays of grapefruit, bacon, eggs, toast, cereal, tea, a hearty repast commensurate with our efforts crossing half the world—that it had not gone entirely unnoticed.

The hostess, dressed I noticed appreciatively in scarlet stilettos, navy and white outfit, tinsel charmingly looped around her neck, slid down the aisle to present us—just as we plummeted through an unexpected burst of turbulence—with certificates.

Let it be known:
On 15 December 2001
Professor Sir Hugo SIR HUGO (Lord Sir Hugo) and
Countess Ruby Rivers (the Countess)
Gained entry into the elevated realm at 32,000 feet
Initiation into the select and privileged circle of
REPUBLICAN
Sensual connoisseurs known as
The Transports of Rapture Club

CONGRATULATIONS!
MAY YOUR DREAMS FLY HIGH WITH
REPUBLICAN!

'Hugo, wake up, we're landing in Hong Kong.'

Ruby's sweet treble voice pierces my dreams. I open my eyes. We're still in our seats. Not a certificate to be seen.

Ruby

Flying into Hong Kong is like flying into a dream I had long ago. The forest of high-rise so close to the airport.

A towering fringe of poverty or imperialism or both.

The tropical heat, humidity presses upon us as we disembark to stroll around the airport, it all feels strangely familiar. Like a pleasurable dream you struggle to hold in mind awake; a name of unknown significance on the tip of one's tongue.

We drink bottles of sickly-sweet water, overpriced coffee at Cabana restaurant. We spend the rest of the fuel stop resting in the first class traveller's lounge; Hugo has a massage. After two hours, we re-board the plane.

The closer it is, less real it seems. There's no turning back now. My path of flight is taking me straight into what I most desire and fear. I breathe into the paper sick-bag. Hugo pats my arm absently, sympathetically, poring over Wittgenstein.

Sydney

Wheels touch ground. The dream connects
The plan proceeds according to plan
Wheels roll, brakes pull back
Jet engines decompress
Passengers shake
Stale crumbs of fear and crumpled dreams
On successful completion
Another passage in their lives
Turning to the New Land
The Old World, the Cold World
Crowds

Greyness of low skies
Film noir seep of black city rain
Away
Brilliant blue mid-morning sky
Sydney in mid-December
Metal glitter
Spears edges, buildings,
Windows,
Lines of heat
Wheels spin fire
—Violent violet dazzle
Walls of airport glass erupt into a golden blaze
The alchemy of
Renaissance dreams
European painters
Gained
Lost
Perspective
In the blink of an
Eye

Hugo

Southern Spiral Hotel, Sydney

Well, yes. I don't think any thinking person could dispute that. I put down Wittgenstein at Ruby's behest and look around me.

'Isn't the view wonderful, Hugo?'

Yes, the view is, hmmm, magnificent. Framed by windows of the Southern Spiral Hotel at Circular Quay, floor nineteen overlooking the harbour. A panorama of light, harbour, sky. A blinding dazzle of light, glittering water traversed by boats: ferries, yachts, billowing spinnakers, red, blue, purple, yellow sails; frothing wake of speedboats, pleasure craft of all descriptions, so much makes one exhausted to look at it. And yonder beyond the Opera House, isn't that the grey periscope of a submarine?

Yes, hmmm, I agree it beats the Thames. And Ruby seems to want to turn cityscape into competition now we are at last here. Her edgy voice impels me to contain thoughts and simply be agreeable. Coughing I light a cigarette, watching her agreeably.

Yes, Sydney Harbour is far more azure than the ancient river that runs through our, my, city. Yes, blasted by laser-light, high-rise, Sugar. O yes, I'm sure you're right. Old buildings are out of sight and we will go to see them soon.

Yes, yes. I agree with my darling who is pacing, unpacking, in such a fetching perplexed tizzy, hunting sunscreen, sunglasses, long-sleeve blouses, trousers, just like an English rose.

Smoke rising, comfortably I walk to the balcony and finish my cigarette. Return to reading on bed, regarding her surreptitiously in between *Remarks on the Philosophy of Psychology.*

I read and images of Ruby slip between the words. I watch, trying to read her thoughts impelling her flurry of unpacking, clothes hanging, bag searching, diary scribbling. I watch her in a fetching perplexing tizzy, through the veil I have no desire to pull away. I love mystery, masks. My attention may be sliding from the written words. But if Ruby were to command:

'Pay Attention!' right now,

I would be at her mercy.

Ruby, Ruby Love. It's too hot for furs here.

But there are feathers, proud, tantalising, teasing.

Golden eagle feathers; her sky-hunter mask.

There are feathers. There is her dress.

Her new dress.

Alluring. Commanding.

In the boldness of its simplicity.

The gift I have, to surprise her with, nestled in its cocoon of pink tissue awaiting the rapture of her gaze, exclamation of delight. The dress hidden in my portmanteau.

A dress of violet silk shall caress her body like water, air.

As if there's nothing there.

Untitled #5

Ruby

We're in Australia but we're not in 'Australia' as I imagined it, not as I'm sure I know it intimately inside of me, part of me, past of me. Not yet, anyway. The hotel suite is impersonal luxury. Suddenly, like Princess X; I think no one would want my life if they knew what was going to happen, but let us not anticipate events. Even when the shadow of death falls across the path do not second-guess the future. Put away the crystal ball! There's no-one more spurned and derided than the 'poor little rich girl'. Don't even have the tough backing of poverty to hold —Hugo— we had been together now— God, I don't know what I am thinking.

Open files. My laptop. Think: art. Art. That's why I'm here, no other reason. Art is my agenda, my whole agenda.

There's nothing hidden in my life.

Hugo is stretched on the bed, philosophical tome beside his sleeping body. Breathing heavily. Snuffling.

Hugo have you found the sweet truffle of dreams? I hope so, baby, if so: Enjoy...

His sleep apnoea terrifies me.

I find myself listening intently, remembering the night he held his breath so long I began kiss-of-life, mouth-to-mouth resuscitation, the last-minute interventions to bring a person back into the land of living.

Then he took an inhalation that rocked the bed.

He wakes up now.

It's afternoon. Still looks very hot out there beyond the privileged realm of air-conditioning. The harbour glistens, as I've not seen it before, or maybe not, perfectly framed in a picture window.

I'm buzzing from the flight but feel strangely empty. With a Do To list as long as a hangover.

Have to, have to, ring my mother and brother in Newcastle. Ha! I joke with Hugo. Leave some flowers on the grave!! The words tumble out of my mouth like a voice in my head, unbidden. He looks at me oddly for a moment, smiles absently and turns back to his book.

I pick up the invitation for the exhibition tomorrow.

Aboriginal/Australian; abstraction, the new landscape of the 21st century.

NEW MILLENNIUM, NEW REPUBLIC at David Yorricks Gallery.

'A large event is planned,' Springer from DYG informed me. 'American movie moguls, the Arts and Culture Ministers and Prime Minister have been invited.'

'What a gathering.' I tickled Hugo's stomach with purple toenails. My husband was lying on the shag-pile carpet clad in crimson yellow-spotted boxers that I gave him for his fifty-sixth birthday this year.

When the engagement was announced there were some who professed it outrageous that he was twenty-five years older than me, I thought there was a pleasing symmetry to it. I admired the shapely puce-painted curves of my toenails against the contrasting chalky-white and mottled-pink flesh-fields of his hairy belly.

'Rhett Felix and Diana Shaw showing in the group show, NEW MILLENNIUM, NEW REPUBLIC—'

The hunting instinct, which propels me rises up. The Art Dealer in me stands, hungry, with a glint in the eye.

I arrange catalogues in a fan on the glass-topped table. It's calling me, the lure of the quarry, the thrill of the chase.

I want to find something rare that no one will believe can exist...

What is that? I say to Hugo.

What?

Did you say something?

No.

I thought I heard a voice?

No I heard nothing. He replies.

I stroll across carpet, imperial blue. Blue as empires overseas. Seas-over empires. Seize the empire.

Illusions of power make me feel better.

A bluegold haze shimmers inciting me... onto the balcony into its irresistible embrace. The air close...stifling... heavy.... a mother I can no longer refuse or deny. It's hard to breathe.

Something is calling. My ears strain to every sound, note, harmony, dis-chord of the evening's music, its magic...

Traffic in the distance moans, the mournful blast of a ferry horn, trains swish on a monorail below... Whirring, clanking, pulsating... The city, this evening, the harbour calling me.

Sydney, the glittering.

Sydney, my city.

I have returned.

Margarita

16, The Mayfair, December 14 2001

I have my own life to look after now. I'm getting back on my feet again and I don't need him hanging around my neck like an albatross dragging me down just to walk all over me again.

I'm the survivor of a relationship 'unfortunate' (I prefer that to 'abusive'). A survivor, surviving, in my apartment in a new life, the apartment George has kindly lent me, whilst he is away overseas for a year on his sabbatical. Yes, his name is George; he works with me in admin at the university, we're in a kind of relationship, his place is on George Street. What's so extraordinary about any of that?

I don't need Raymond. Shouldn't have agreed to meet him at the MCA next to the Harbour after work yesterday; but he sounded down and pitiful on the phone, so repentant, I went, thinking I could cheer him up with tales of the cicada.

'Marge you're cracking girl. But what d'you expect with all that violin playing?'

He stirred spoons of sugar into his cup, slopping froth. He wasn't looking helpless in his beaten-up black leather jacket, paint-splattered jeans, work boots. I thought he looked cute: red hair flying erratically from his head; typical pallor; sharp angles of his bone structure, nose, jaw, brow; mocking mouth, pale blue eyes behind his glasses.

I looked away from him. I had made a conscious decision to ignore veiled pleas; need, the hurt I saw in his eyes, heard in the tenor of his voice; dependency, which kept me running around in circles for him, doing everything for him, for years.

I watched a ferry glide into the quay in a froth of wake. A

girl in a pink dress chasing pigeons. I listened to the roar of the city, laughter from a nearby table, a mother's voice calling kindly to a daughter, Lindy, let's get an ice-cream.

And I said, 'no. Ray. I'm not going. I don't care who's there. I have things to do.'

And with that I stood up walked away. Leaving him to pay.

Raymond

Alchemy Studios, Matraville, December 14

—Could have hurled it against a wall, broken its bloody neck——through rehab, did a lot, yeah. But she wanted to be there, and I had a lot of crap too—

—had enough of —'looking after me'—

—I went off drinking—

—when I've been broke, now that Margarita's left me—

—reaction to medication he'd prescribed, which sent me off the loop—

—Margarita when she jumped ship. All I could do—

—there after all, it was on offer. I never did quite—

—number. He said ring, go and see him, any time I like. He's a decent bloke a—

—I restrained myself, every time. Instead I went out, picked fights with drunk-fucks—

—Bitch who does she think she is. Margarita... I was never interested in her in the first—

—with my old painting mates—

—a hole in your life—

—After all, it wasn't love. I never told her I loved her

—as she so insultingly put it. It's true she helped me

—reached Wealth Bank, when the officers stopped me.

Two of them. 'Hey son'—

—He even got me off charge the cops were pressing. They wanted me in—

—million pieces—   —that violin playing—

—I ended up in hospital unconscious. Marge had to come to take me home—

—didn't get it that I was supposed to treat as if she were—

—I am searching for something so rare—

—Sometimes I talk with him five times a week. Keeps me on the rails. He's even lent me money—

—so beautiful—

—I walked down George Street, Sydney, kicking in all the shop windows—

—no one will believe—

—jail. But Jeffrey Bellow stood up in court and said that I was having an allergic—

—some kind of Love Goddess

—can exist—

Ruby

Southern Spiral Hotel, Sydney, December 14

Hugo and I spend our day in Sydney mostly in a hotel room. Early in the morning he awakens me with a gift. A pink box, his hands tremble.

'Early Christmas present, Darling,' he says.

Beneath his unruly curls streaked with grey, my husband is handsome, face radiating an expression of anticipation. I smile graciously, feeling that I should rather be asleep.

I lift the lid, part layers of pink tissue, and unfold a violet silk dress.

'Oh, Hugo. It's beautiful!' I exclaim

I must exaggerate voice, smile, and delight in my eyes, and put on a perfect pitched performance. Exude! It wouldn't do to be low-key with Hugo; dramatic statement, theatrical gesture, is all. I have to enact my pleasure.

'What an absolutely beautiful dress!' I hold it up against me. Stroke the exquisite violet silk, antique lace. Hugo is still trying to get me out of 'Mrs P.M. business suits' as he puts it.

'I thought you'd like it darling,' he says shyly, 'I thought you could wear it here. Get you out of your power shoulders.'

His blue-grey eyes shine. He gives me the second part of my costume. And now I understand what he wants.

'The Headdress,' he hands me a gold and turquoise Egyptian-looking helmet.

For a while now, he has mentioned his Cleopatra fantasy. In a past life he imagines he was a slave on the Nile. One day he was spotted by the stately queen who took time from her royal duties surveying river work, to trample his back as he lay prostrate on the riverbank; her strong bare feet with long toenails pushing him deep into the squelching black mud of the delta...

When eventually we left the hotel mid-afternoon to 'take the air' as Hugo puts it I was wearing my dress. I would have preferred to wear something more concealing to protect my skin from intense ultra-violet rays. The fragile fabric was so delicate it was nearly transparent, underneath it I wore a cream silk slip. Still, the situation was unusual, I felt attached to Hugo, almost dependent on him, as I leaned on his arm in that oh-so-feminine dress and we strolled around the Rocks like any happy tourist couple, window shopping.

Hugo

That day remains etched in memory in a black frame of grief. Grief that does not so much as dissolve but fades to hardest steely grey; as the vast ocean of Time washes me away from that static frozen point in time, from the hardness of submerged rocks, the treacherous Australian reef that sank our ship, my unsuspecting boat of ruby Ruby love.

Ruby

Southern Spiral Hotel, 14 December 2001

I had my itinerary planned. I didn't want any free time, any spaces, or any gaps in my timetable. Gaps are dangerous you can fall through gaps. And there was much to do. Rhett Felix. Gary Doyle. Burudyara. I repeated artists' names in my mind like a mantra. I reckoned, with my business acumen, that if I aimed for four with confidence, I might capture at least two. I sat on the hotel-suite sofa. I'd brought the Sugar manilla folder, reading in between conversations in the plane.

Hugo talking about the fallacy that we can't convey what we feel and mean in writing. 'We transmit emotions in body language yet we convey feelings in words in writing and when expressed together, in our dramas,' he raised his eyebrow meaningfully.

That sounded self-evident not nonsensical to me at that present time.

As Hugo talked, I looked out the window, lulled, gazing at clouds blaze pink-and-gold like a fresco by Bernini in the afternoon sky over planet Earth.

As Hugo's persuasive tones boomed I remembered that long ago when Margarita and I were only fourteen and hadn't known each other very long Margarita, precocious, argumentative, provocative, asked the question that later I was to read in philosophy books.

'How do you know that what I see is red is what you see as 'red'?' 'Is a person A at time X the same as person A at time Y?'

And I had no answer, impressed by the precociousness of the ideas. There was an element of competition between us; vying to gain knowledge, sets you free I believed, then the object of our search shifted to the opposite sex.

Boys. Men.

The nature of that knowledge was emotional-physical, it seemed the two were intertwined.

Margarita once said: 'I would never commit suicide. If life became so bad I want to end it, I'd move somewhere else, begin a new life, do what I wanted to, become another person, someone who I wanted to be...'

But it was me who left, who must have believed it. Me who became the person in a different life.

And I could reply to Margarita now: great idea baby, but life is not so easy as you may imagine when you are seventeen and never worn a Cleopatra headdress or sky-hunter mask.

My life is good, but it's complicated; I'm digressing, allowing my thoughts to dart off all over the place.

I pick up the artist file folders, turn to what's in hand. Tonight's opening at DYG. Although Springer from the gallery rang me I must ring Yorricks to let him know we've arrived.

It is late when we eventually leave the hotel.

The city is glowing, an unearthly sinister golden light. On the hotel radio we heard about bushfires outside the city. As we leave the hotel the air crackles with a strange static.

'My heavens look at the sky,' exclaims Hugo.

Black and red fire clouds billow over the city skyline from south to north; the ash filled sky is like a vision of hell.

Untitled #6

Forest Floor

On the way to a northern NSW rainforest

Several years before

I arrived in the middle of the night. I'd taken the northbound train up the coast from Sydney known as 'the hippie train'. Despite never having been there I was still confident I would somehow find my way to your cousin's place. I had the address from twenty-page letters you'd been sending me.

As the train neared Grafton we passed through kilometres of black flying bats, massive fruit bats with wing spans of two metres or more. The evening sky was seething, stippled with shrieking winged bodies, a cloud of bats. I leaned from the open window of the train with the warm tropical wind pulling my hair staring into a mesh of thousands of bombarding horror film silhouettes Dracula's friends screaming like a thousand infants being slaughtered. Except these were not vampire bats. They lived on fruit sugar.

I was thrilled by the exotic strangeness of it. The adventure. The power of taking my destiny into my hands, but going with my arrival unannounced. On my own.

I'd left Margarita at Mother's house, with her violin (booked in to a Psychic Healing Workshop). I had shorts, tee shirts, books, towel and sleeping bag in my backpack. My airline bag was filled with writing and painting things. Decaffeinated coffee, apples; Rimbaud.

I was prepared to stay for as long as it felt right.

The train arrived at the station as night was falling. I stepped onto the platform, stood for a moment, looked around. Only one other passenger had disembarked. A tall fit-looking man with a beard talking jovially with a large man with a long beard, dressed in blue he looked like the stationmaster, cheerful voices echoed in the thickening dusk. I assumed they must know each other.

I pulled a scrap of paper with Ray's cousin's address from the front pocket of my jeans shorts, well; I guessed I would have to set off to… wherever it was.

I walked out of the station and stopped again.

In front of me was an almost empty car park, sloping up to a road. Beyond the road, a fringe of dark tall trees. A few wooden houses on high stilt legs. Sub-tropical outer suburbia.

There were no shops. No people in sight. The cloudy sky was purple-black, air warm and close with humidity. The screeching bats ripped electrically through the stillness.

I turned and looked back to the lights and movement of the station.

The bearded man I'd noticed talking to the stationmaster was I saw walking purposefully towards the only vehicle in the car park, a white four-wheel drive.

Clutching my piece of paper, I strode quickly.

'Excuse me, do you know how to get to—' I glanced at the piece of paper, 'Styx Creek?' I smiled with determined charm.

He paused, his hand on the car door.

'Styx Creek?' He repeated the name slowly.

'Yes, I'm going to a friend's place. But I've never been there before I don't know how to get there. Do you know where I could get a bus?'

He looked doubtful.

'You won't get a bus there. Buses don't go there. It's right out in the forest.'

'The forest?' I thought of Little Red Riding Hood.

'You're going to a friend's place?' He said looking at me.

'Yes, that's right. I've just come up from Sydney.'

His face tightened in sudden resolution.

'Well I can take you out that way if you want. I'm going in that direction, some way towards it, anyhow.'

He unlocked his four-wheel drive, and I stepped into the seat. Taking a lift from a stranger didn't cost me a thought I told myself. I'd been hitching alone since I was young, you develop the instinct for who's okay, and who's not. But this was all part of the adventure. There was no other way I could have got out there.

'I'm Tony, by the way,' he said as we left the town behind us.

'Rosamond,' I turned to look at him, 'pleased to meet you.'

Tony wanted to know the details of my journey. Where had I come from? Who was I visiting? I had been hitching since I was thirteen, and I had worked out a hitchhiker's bargain. Talk with willed psychic strength that is protection so that (I prayed) no-one not even a maniac could think dangerous thoughts. It was a roulette of terror and faith. The last recourse of one with no transport. Praying my guardian angel is not off-duty.

It was much further from Grafton than I'd thought.

When we were a few kilometres out of the town we passed an intersection.

'That's my turn-off.' Tony tilted his head. 'I'll drive you a bit further out, though,' he added.

We reached a turn off into an unsealed road.

'It's down this direction,' said Tony. After he'd been driving for what seemed like a long time Tony was getting upset. Rocks kept flying up from the dirt track hitting the underside of the vehicle. I could hear them pinging erratically, each one sounded louder than the one before as if under increasing attack from the track.

'My petrol tank could get punctured,' he sounded irritated.

'Where is it? We must have reached it by now...' He was sounding slightly angry now.

'Well, it says just after Styx Creek, there should be a gate on the right,' I squinted at a drawing Ray had given me in Sydney.

Tony was clearly a decent kind of guy. Not the type to leave a girl in the middle of a forest in the middle of the night, alone. At least, that's what I hoped. The tension was growing sharper.

Eventually we drove across a shallow creek, right of which I could just make out bars of a farm gate.

Tony stopped. The headlights picked out a field. But there were no lights, no dwelling to be seen.

'Well, thank you,' I said. 'That was great I don't know what I would have done—' I started to open the car door.

'I'll take you there,' said Tony.

'It's okay, I'm sure I can find it from here.'

I was excited about surprising Ray. I didn't care whether this bearded kind Samaritan took me to the door or not.

'No, no, I'll take you there,' he insisted.

I jumped out, opened the gate, which he drove through. I closed the gate and climbed back in. The headlights extended in funnels of light down a dip in the field and then up again.

There was no road or track and we drove in the darkness up and over a hillock.

Now I could see a light shining in the dark, from a window.

I remembered Ray had said his cousin and his wife were living in a barn they had built themselves. One day they'd build a house.

As we drove towards the building, a wild bearded figure ran out waving a shotgun.

'YAAAHHH!! Waddayawanfucker?? Stop there!! Fuck off bastards, fuck off or I'll kill ya!!! I'll fuckin kill ya!!!'

He was pointing a shotgun straight at us. A man with a big dark beard dressed in overalls.

'Christ!' Tony said softly. I stared through the windscreen with interest. Ray had said that his cousin was wild.

'That must be Rex, my friend's cousin.'

'Your friend's cousin—who is your friend anyway?'

I opened the door and climbed out, calling loudly as I did so.

'Hello! Rex! Rex? You must be Rex?'

'I'm Rosamond—a friend of Ray's—is Ray here?'

'What?' The wild bearded man lowered his gun staring at me, looking bewildered.

'Rosamond? You're Rosamond? You're looking for Ray?'

'Yes,' I said, walking towards him.

'I'm sorry I didn't get in touch before I got here. I know it's a bit unexpected. Is Ray here?'

'Nita, Anita!!' Rex called back into the door of the barn.

'Rosamond's here! It's Rosamond! Rosamond's here!'

'Come in! Come in!' Rex said.

'Ray's down at the shack, down the track. We'll go down

there in a few minutes...'

When we were in the barn Ray's cousin asked, 'who's this?'

'Tony,' he stepped forward hand outstretched.

'Fuck off,' said Rex, stepping back with a sneer.

I was surprised Tony stayed, but stayed he did, eagerly sharing joints of home-grown that Rex rolled, talking with Nita, he accompanied us as we all set off to Ray's shack.

We walked in single file along the track down a hill, lantern swinging in Rex's hand, through forest trees, around bushes.

Towards a distant light shining in the forest. We stepped on stones over a splashing creek, walked over another track around a bend and there he was, my lover.

Ray, stumbling out of the shack, wearing nothing but a pair of blue shorts, blinking, looking puzzled, rumpled, like a creature disturbed in its hibernation.

Rex and Nita were smiling broadly as if sharing a big joke. 'Ray, Ray-you-old-bastard, look who's here...'

'You've got a visitor!'

'What are you doing here?' Ray was staring as if he literally could not believe his eyes. As if I were some kind of apparition.

'I just happened to be in the area and thought I'd drop in and visit,' I said, airily, just managing to keep a straight face.

Later he said he believed my joke, that he actually thought I had just happened to be driving through the rainforest outside Grafton in the middle of night, hundreds of miles north of home in Sydney and decided to call in to visit him. He said he thought Tony was my latest boyfriend.

And nothing I could say or do to convince him otherwise had any real effect.

Diary entry

Day 2

Early morning. Lost track of day and date. Decide to have a swim in the river. Walk through the forest. Past a half-built house on stilts. Ray said it belongs to an architect who comes every few months to construct the house. There is a rainwater tank there where we fill bottles, it's closer than Rex and Nita's barn.

Sensual swim—feel like a combination of Ophelia, Lady Godiva, and the Lady of Shallots— abandon self to sensation, drifting, eyes closed, floating on the surface of green water in sunlight. Pull myself onto the riverbank. Dripping sunshine. Walk the track. Delicious feeling of walking in fragrant forest, river-washed skin, caressed by warm air. I spy Ray filling a bottle. He looks up.

We haven't yet slept together these past nights.

We have lain zipped up in sleeping bags on opposite sides of the shack. Testing a concept of single sleeping bag as full-body chastity belt.

Ray has been going to bed later than me. Working late every night behind a wall in a concealed space with shelves and bench at the back of the shack. We've both been waking early, as the first rays of light slide in. He lights a fire on the earth floor in a fireplace surrounded by stones, puts the pan to boil on a grid balanced on bricks in the fire. The sofa is an old car seat, with spring coils sticking through torn vinyl, on the ground.

We sit. He drinks rum. I drink decaffeinated coffee. Then he goes into the back of the shack to work.

I have been living on decaffeinated coffee, powdered milk, eating apples. Trying to be healthy, and detox in the country.

Ray's diet is as restricted: rum, dark chocolate, home-grown, and magic mushrooms from the forest, from what he's told me. None since I have been here.

Now and then he walks out to consult the book he brought with him, *Food of Gods,* an illustrated study of humanity's relationship with natural intoxicants and hallucinogens.

Day 4

Rex drove Ray and I to Grafton in his ute, went to a dim cafe with an overhead fan that is broken, goes whirr whirr clunk, as it spins. Ray described it in one of his letters, he made it sound like the most perversely desirable place in the world to visit. The bored waitresses, those poor wretches, the awesome burden of life...We went to a supermarket; I bought cheese, crispbread, lettuce and apples. He bought steak. Drove back to the forest.

He's preoccupied with what he's working on, rarely leaves the concealed space at the back. I hear him: Trying to find something rare, beautiful, no one will believe it can exist... I haven't felt like drinking overproof rum with Ray. He's been unsympathetic. I have withdrawn from him. But I'm happy to see him more than happy. Right here, right now.

'Hi,' I say.

'Yep,' he replies.

'Do you want to go up into the house?' I say smiling at him.

I follow him up the ladder. He lies on the floorboards. I lie on top of him.

His body hardens. Freezes—beneath me. He turns away. 'What's wrong?' I ask. "Don't you feel like making love, darling?' Aware of the sarcasm in my voice.

'No, I don't. And I'm not going to.'

'What?'

He's pulling on his tee shirt, face pale. Looking serious.

'You don't mean it?' 'Yes I do. It's not right.'

'What are you talking about: not right?'

'I'm waiting for the right woman.' He's pulling on his shorts.

'The right woman?"

I stare at him in disbelief. What about the letters he sent in the last weeks to me at my mother's house in Sydney proclaiming his love. Everything that's happened between us?

Then I remember. Whatshisname. 'You don't really think I was with that guy do you? I was hitching. How many times do I have to tell you—'

But he is bending down and picking up the water bottle.

'I'm going back to the hut.'

I watch him disappearing through the trapdoor. Feet first, legs, torso, shoulders, lastly his head topped by wicked flame-red locks.

Bye-bye baby.

I sit in the unfinished room, skeletal bones of hope. One day the architect—he? she?—will have a house. Sounds drift.

Bird song. River plashes. Joists, naked frames, plasterboards piled in a stack. Out in nature's paradise, walls are going up everywhere.

Arise, Maiden of the Forest-Morning. Sweep sawdust from skin. Descend through trapdoor. Time enough for him to return. Not following him. Walk slowly back along forest track. Little red riding person without a woodcutter to save her. He's not worth it anyway. Whatever did I see in him?

After I risked my life to find him.

I had been prepared to stay as long as it felt right and now it was time to pack up and leave. It would not take long. A few bits of food, books. Rimbaud—a selection. *Gold of the Tigers* by Borges. I sit on a bough on the packed earth floor of the shack, open Rimbaud at random.

They leave, forgetting that their flesh prickles
Where the Priest of Christ laid his forceful claws.
The Priest is provided with the shaded roof of a bower [12]
Well, I would leave, forgetting my flesh.

Leave Ray beneath the shaded roof of his arbour.

Shouldering my backpack of dreams, hitching fortune to the endless afternoon, and just hope I'll get a lift.

I slide the books into the backpack, with my journal, coffee and water bottle I filled at the house. The cheese, bread, lettuce. I'd eaten all the apples.

Ray was, just for a change, working in his studio at the back of the shack.

I walked to the doorway, and looked in at him. Bent over one of his elaborate geometric sketches. I wondered, what was he doing? I didn't see much evidence of his heroic metaphysical quest.

A few drawings; rubbish he'd found on the forest floor. Tins, wrappers that he had nailed onto the makeshift walls. A counterpart to collages of leaves pinned to the wall of his garage in Adelaide that I'd been so taken by, many months ago. That's all I could see in the small space that he rarely left.

'I'm going to go.'

I stood in the doorway staring at his back.

Naked torso, pink-white skin, blue shorts, hair irradiated by sunbeams filtering through the window, and cracked walls… 'I said, I'm GOING TO GO.'

'Waa—' he spun around looking dazed and bemused.

'Go? Where?"

Sydney.' I gazed past him out the window at grass between trees. Irradiated in dazzling light, glowing as if lit within. Who could ever need drugs to unlock their doors of perception here? Someone with perception deficit, I think. I give my ex-lover a controlled hard glare.

Untitled #7

You're going? When?'

'Today. Now. No time like the present. The train to Sydney leaves at six. I'll walk to the main road. Hitch to Grafton.'

He's looking at me as if he can't believe it.

But what else did he think I would do? What else could a girl do, after 'I'm waiting for the right woman'?

Untitled #8

He walked with me to the road to Grafton, seven kilometres down the dirt track winding through the forest. We didn't talk. The air seemed increasingly thin, insubstantial, as if losing its heavy hypnotic hold the further away I walked. I was glad of the chance to really walk somewhere. Stretch my legs. The track became sealed road before it reached the highway. He stopped at the exact point where it met the tarmac.

'Well, I'll leave you here, skipper,' Ray said. 'Hope you get a lift alright.'

'I will,' I said. 'Bye.'

And that was that.

He turned around and started to walk back into the forest.

I turned abruptly and walked on alone. Trying to tell myself I felt better the further away from him I walked. Why was everything confusing, difficult? I was following advice, making a firm decision and sticking to it, acting as if uncertainty, chaos, could be resolved by taking action. But it wasn't working, I was walking away from Ray and all I felt was empty.

A line from one of his letters ran through my head.

An instant of Nothingness expands to soul-consuming proportions.

It's not so bad I tried to convince myself.

You've only lost the love of your life.

Light of your days and nights.

Ha! I gazed resolutely across the paddocks coming into view, reaching a clearing.

I stopped when I reached the road. I did not have a watch.

After what seemed like a long while, I heard a car. A white sedan sped into view around the bend in the road. I held out my arm, smiling, willing it to stop. It sped by obliviously.

An unmeasured period of time expanded into itself as I sat on the grass at the side of the road.

The rumble of an engine approached from the west.

A truck came into view; I jumped up waving my upturned thumb. It swerved to a stop a few metres in front of me, and I ran towards it.

Two young blonde guys were sitting in the high cabin. The long-haired passenger opened his door.

'Where ya goin'?' he called down.

'I'm going to Grafton,' I called back up.

'You can ride in the back if you want, there's no room up here.'

'Okay, thanks,' I said, picking up my backpack.

'Sure you want to go in there?' He asked with a big smile.

I glanced around me at the back of the small truck.

'Yeah,' I replied, why wouldn't I?

He jumped down, I followed him to the back of the small container truck. He opened the pull-down door. I could see it was empty, dark.

'You sure you'll be alright there?' He was looking at me oddly, as if there was an undertone to the question.

It wasn't going to be very comfortable but it was only forty kilometres I figured. If I didn't take this lift, I'd probably miss the train. 'Yeah, I'll be fine,' I said.

'If you're not okay, just give us a yell and we'll stop.' He was still looking at me quizzically as if it was a challenge.

I scrambled up into the container, which was about a metre from the ground. He grimaced in a strange smile.

'Okay,' I said, brightly.

The truck door slammed shut. It was impossible to not

know what the vehicle was used for. The smell of fish was nauseating.

As the truck drove off I could feel every bump magnified as if the truck had no suspension.

There seemed to be a succession of craters in the road surface which rattled the truck jarring my spine. But that was nothing. Before long— faint, dizzy, panting as if I'd run for miles, gasping for air—I realized it must be a sealed container.

Every breath I took was depleting a limited oxygen supply. I crawled over the floor to the cabin-end, made a fist and banged the wall of the metal container.

'Hello! Help! Please Stop The Truck!!' Nothing happened. Of course they wouldn't be able to hear me above the roar of the engine. They must have known that, and known there was no air in here.

I would surely die when the oxygen ran out. How long would that take? Not long judging by how dizzy I felt. So this was how my life would end. In an insulated fish truck on the road to Grafton. It didn't seem right.

Crawled back, I slumped, gazing forward. My eyes were drawn to a dot of light, a minute crack letting in light in the thick black rubber seal around the door.

A pinhole. Where there is light there must be air, I reasoned. Gathering all my strength, I took out my pen, pushed its tip into the hole, and poked and pulled until it tore, then I put my mouth right on the tear in the seal and breathed in greedily. Air! That's how I kept breathing all the way. Thanking the power of my pen for widening an airway. Thanking a pinhole, a crack, for my chance to keep breathing, stay alive

Eventually the truck ground and shuddered to a halt.

The door was pulled open. I reeled with the impact of

light, air, LIFE! The land of the living. The same blonde guy watching me suspiciously, laughing as if at some big private joke—had he really tried to kill me?

'Okay?' He was peering at me darkly.

'Yes,' I almost fell and staggered onto terra firma.

'Thanks for the lift.' Calling his bluff. I'd got here, that was all that mattered now.

The truck had pulled up opposite the railway station, next to the car park. At almost exactly the same place I'd set off in the bearded man's four-wheel drive, to find Ray, six days ago.

Untitled #9

Well, one part of mission impossible had been completed, had I known how hard the other part would be, and that there even was another part, I would not have bothered. Maybe I had taken too much for granted but given the letters of love he had sent and what had happened between us before that, I did not think it unreasonable to assume as I had that he would be glad to see me.

As I walked down hill to the station every step I took felt as if I were bouncing on a trampoline. The stench of fish remained in my nostrils for hours after I was comfortably ensconced on the southbound train, bottle of Railways burgundy before me, trying to forget everything that had happened. My dream lover. Cynicism deepened, took hold, a process of a self-deception. I was on my way back to join Margarita, waiting for me at Mum's house, an eager recipient of bad news on the relationship front.

*

After I returned Margarita would hardly say a word to me, let alone look at me. Only when I reassured her that Ray and I had split up, it was a disaster, we hadn't got on, does she begin to cheer up and relent just a fraction.

'I find him repulsive,' I felt I had to say as we sat out on the veranda. An image of his back turned against me flashed into my thoughts. 'He has soft arms.'

She gives me an odd look. But she's beginning to relax. The more I assure her that I'm not seeing him again, the quicker her mood improves. Far from commiserating, expressing sympathy that my love has ended, let alone suggesting I try to work things out with him, instead the more details I can let out against him, the happier my friend appears. She looked as if she might smile and talk to me again—soon. If I only say a few horrible things about him.

I don't tell her the real reason I left. I just say I no longer find him attractive. Now when she spends her hours playing violin, I felt there was not so much a wall between us as a veil, which I could easily part, if I wanted to.

I sat on the terrace next to Aphrodite's latest water feature, a lion's head spouting a foaming aqua jet from yawning jaws, splashing noisily from authentically aged brick. She walked out.

'I think I will do classical violin again,' she announced, but she didn't look at me.

'You know I played in the Glebe Youth Orchestra until I was thirteen that is until just before I met you.'

I was surprised at the edge of accusation in her voice.

'You weren't playing violin when I first met you, when we arrived at the school,' I said.

What was she trying to say?

'Surely you're not implying there was a connection between my arrival at school, and your giving up classical violin. If so it would have had to have been one of reverse causality, as if my arrival into your life caused Time to go backwards.'

'Grandpa taught me from when I was three.'

I looked at her long slender musical fingers holding a crystal goblet in which she was swirling vodka and tonic.

I didn't tell her that I had also stopped playing. I had played descant recorder in the Youth Choir in Beijing, an instrument of Baroque music. Yet I had all but forgotten, it had sunk far from my mind. I had always wanted to play violin but never had the chance.

A few nights later I asked Margarita to go to Adelaide with

me. I was heading back to do my second year at university.

'Okay,' she said. 'But you'd better not change your mind.'

'I'm never having anything to do with that creep again.'

*

I had a guilty secret. Every morning I rose from my big bed, brewed strong coffee, sat at the table in the kitchenette, trying not to touch asbestos-fibro walls with my legs and disturb the lethal fibres.

I looked at my reflection in the window. My ghost-pale face framed by long hair. I had seen his work, could not forget it, I saw it in my mind, and was filled with yearning for what I did not know, for what had not happened, yet which would not let me go. The colour field studies that he made before he went to the rainforest, called out to me.

I had looked deeply into Raymond Furness's work, the grids and bars, illusory geometric forms, which in my eyes did not entrap, did not stop there; instead, seeming to bend before my gaze, twisting, changing, giving way to endlessly recurring optical patterns, paths, possibilities; letting me into an altered state of reality, a colour field of vision. The feeling of excitement it gave me was like the illusion of finding a colour that only he and I could see.

I gazed through the window not seeing the leaves, and trees below. I did not see tangled undergrowth; intensely blue Adelaide sky. All I saw were memories, scenarios unfolding in the theatre of my imagination where Margy could not see what I was thinking.

I saw Ray working in his shack, in the rainforest, where I left him. My thoughts starting as a trickle grew into a torrent. I was dreaming him so intensely; it must be reciprocal. Was I dreaming him or he dreaming me?

105

It could not be possible that it was over, not when I still felt this way about him.

As the days passed I felt him entering my consciousness, like the excitation of a magnetic field as a magnet draws near.

Margy and I went for a walk along the beach from Glenelg to Brighton and back one brilliant blue-skied afternoon. As we reached the Esplanade at Brighton, I saw him. A wrenchingly familiar figure, dressed in black, sloping past the bottle shop.

'Furness!' Margarita shouted.

I was surprised that she would want to attract his attention; after all she'd said. How much she didn't want me to have anything more to do with him.

We approached each other. Margarita and I walking barefooted up from sand. Ray walking down from the street. I felt danger crackling like the smell of sulphur in the salt sea air.

'Sure, Furness what are you doin' here, boyo?' Margarita said in her mock Irish accent.

He cackled, softly.

'You came back from the rainforest.'

I looked into his blue eyes.

He looked back at me.

And I felt myself starting to fall.

Ruby

The Rocks, evening, December 14

'My, my, look at that sky, says Hugo. The sharpness, the edge of the exhilaration of arrival that I had felt just hours ago dissipated into an ominous reality. Suddenly the sky had turned angry, elemental. Red and black fire-clouds were right above the city.

Hugo is wearing a white suit, rose-pink shirt with a white collar, and darker rose silk tie. I am wearing the violet frock, covered by a shawl not because the barometer dropped but as it makes me feel less self-conscious to wear more.

We walk, fingers entwined, and stand on the curb. The cab screeches to a halt. Hugo holds the door; I climb in, placing my black leather laptop case gently on the floor. Only as we stepped into the gallery did I realize I had left my laptop case in the cab. I turned to Hugo in dismay, as the taxi disappeared into traffic gridlocking the streets of Surry Hills. I didn't have a mobile to call the cab company whose phone number advertised on the taxi door, I memorised as it drove off. What an inauspicious arrival into the Sydney art world. And things were only going to dramatically worsen. Although in private life, depending on which way you looked at it what was to happen next was no less than a miracle, the answer to my dreams, spinning at thirty-two feet per second, the speed at which bodies fall.

Hugo

Was prepared to meet the Prime Minister. More than up to it, I am used to meeting heads of state. Although my position of authority has dwindled since our chaps were ousted by the rabble-rousers last election, similar state of affairs existing here since, bringing the loonies in another term. But, as at home, it is my duty to meet and greet as an Englishman abroad knows how. I'll play the game for Ruby, with the greatest of pleasure.

Ruby

Went into the gallery, met David Yorricks and asked to use his phone to ring the taxicab company, told they would ring back when the cab had been traced when they did ring when the opening was in full swing it was to say there was no trace of my case. By then I'd had the privilege of meeting the prime minister. Seen Felix's abstract grids of loss that drew the eye.

A broken compass hovering towards Home and… Words for a catalogue essay forming imperceptibly, eyes swam searching found much to say yes to, themes of identity loss, dislocation, resonating—or was it just the wine, the heat, jet lag, affecting me?

'Zhou, Countess Ruby Rivers from London.'

David Yorricks was waving his arms expansively.

'I love your red, wonderful shade.'

I took a deep sip of purple Shiraz.

'In China, red is symbolic. It stands for the family, for life, considered good luck in houses, everyone puts up red things.'

Words threaded in and out of hearing. I smiled and nodded, eyes swinging from paintings, installations, to searching the crowd. Doing my opening night show shuffle, weaving in and out, only vaguely aware of Hugo at the sliding periphery of my vision, locked in head-bent conversation with the prime minister. I turned towards a wall of Gary Doyle's at the end, and it happened.

I saw him.

Untitled #10

I looked up. My eyes met his.

Raymond.

He was walking from a room into the main gallery. Dressed in lime-green trousers, canary shirt, red sandals; red shock of hair around his head. I see isolated piece-by-piece details in retrospect, individual idiosyncratic details that I registered in a heart-stopping soul-pumping moment of shock—

Ray?
It can't be.
Ray. Oh my god it is—
Ray.

His eyes—mouth curving in a smile of recognition.

Smiling with what I imagine to be charm but which probably looks like what it is—grappling for my last moment of the disappearing social world. 'I've just seen somebody I have to catch!' I head off ducking and weaving through the throng.

I move towards him like a sleepwalker. Hypnotised.

He's looking at me as if he can't believe his eyes either.

Raymond

I am

searching for

SOMETHING

so

rare

& Beautiful

No one

will

believe

it can

exist

Ruby

I was looking at an old parchment map yellowed with age. As I gazed into the black wiggle of coastline, the dark points of cities, all of a sudden I was there in that dream world; sea blue; fresh hair-tossing wind, big white sails cracking above me. The clipper ship sped towards a coastline; port came rushing up, opened to greet the ship in the mouth of a canal.

And then I was sailing in a smaller boat a gondola, down a canal lined with stonewalls over which tumble colourful flowers.

And you are beside me, my love, as we speed onwards and inwards, glorious as a king and a queen in a fairy tale taking the angles of the ancient oriental city in golden light.

The gondola is stopping. I am ascending a flight of steps into crowds of smiling people, traditional dress, long pigtails, chattering.

Courteous citizens lead me to an inn. The building is big; I enter a hall, accompanied up stairs through several wooden rooms. Ascending swiftly, each room is smaller and darker than the one before.

I enter the room at the top of the inn. Tiny, dark, tucked in like a womb doubled-over to fit no room to move I curl up. Knowing I will never return.

Hugo

Talking with the Prime Minister about what happened in the Sixties when we had our first wave of what was called third world immigration, when I realised I couldn't see Ruby. Over the hour we'd been in the gallery if we weren't together, I had kept her in my sight. My eyes restlessly swept the sea of strangers. I had a terrible sinking feeling, a dull panic, a kind of fear as if somehow I knew something terrible had befallen or was about to befall, my love.

Margarita

16, The Mayfair, George Street, Sydney

When does it start, the dark wordless urge to end it; when does it start, the decay in the heart of love?

I loved him, and thought that he loved me. Maybe I made the naïve mistake of confusing physicality with love, in the early days, as if love overflowed from an orgasm. And it was more than a physical relationship for him. I know from the way he still keeps coming back. Despite that we are supposed to have split up. I know from the ties he wraps around me, drawing tighter and tighter until I feel I cannot breathe; he's going to cut me with his chains and burdens, shackles of pain, uncertainties, fears. He is still dependent on me.

We arrived in Sydney five years ago. We'd been together five years, seems impossible looking back that it could ever have felt so good, so thrilling, and fun. But it did.

When it first started illicitly, a feather whispering over tantalizing planes and dips of skin in the depths of night.

In the house of love.

A masked intruder whose caresses you silently but urgently invite. Willing his dangerous advances upon you.

The thing you could do! When Rosa was here, with Ray. Margarita was ever persistent and practical in the apartment they shared in the Castle they called it, and I admit I would try. We moved as Adelaide had become small. Ringed in by small-minded hypocrisy as he said. I was on Ray's side. I admired his guts, his 'battle against the bourgeoisie' although I didn't join. I helped him and friends when they painted their murals of social justice heroes on the walls of buildings in the city at night.

Paintings of Che, Nelson Mandela, Martin Luther King, and Aboriginal activists, Charlie Perkins, with borders of red, yellow, and black Aboriginal flags.

I picked him up, nursed his drunken head in taxis, bringing him home from parties, when he could hardly stand.

In some ways being with Ray reminded me of the years with her. She'd moved from Beijing where her father worked.

There was one main difference between us though. Rosa became obsessed with love. She bought a heterosexual myth: that having a relationship with the 'right' kind of boy or man is a pinnacle of achievement that brought happiness and joy to life—a prized ideal—check the teenage girls' and women's press, it's the same. I tried to pump up my interest to match hers, had to, or could not have been her best friend.

Rosa was restless. She seemed to have limitless energy. Not to mention testosterone, whatever is the hormone supposed to fuel libido... She found it hard to sleep. By the time we were sixteen, going out, most of our nocturnal escapades were conducted under a cloak of secrecy and subterfuge—which to me was the adventure—had become a main drive of her existence. This was supposed to help in her aim to be an artist. In a twist of Rosa-logic I couldn't follow she professed that love-lust for life, and the art-urge were inextricably intertwined; and she had a theory that she delighted in relaying: sexuality was the life-spring well from which works of artistic genius were intuitively drawn. She'd reel off a list of artist lovers: Picasso, Renoir, Caravaggio, Frieda Kahlo, Anna Akhmatova, Anäis Nin, Francis Bacon, Jeff Koons, as evidence to support her original Theory of Art.

Despite different backgrounds Rosa and I got on, we were both different. We felt like Outsiders in a school for Outsiders as if we recognized each other. It wasn't that Rosa expressed what I felt, she didn't. It wasn't so much that I wanted to be like her, I didn't. I liked to be involved, to be with her in her ethical battles and dramas and there was always something that was driving her to eloquence and action. Some theory or idea she was arguing as if someone's life depended on it. Rosa was on a roller coaster of self-conviction but it was not boring being with her. 'When you're famous, they'll be sorry,' I said, imagining a future in which I would continue to play a major supporting role as she became renowned, boldly forging her radical artistic path against the odds, it made me feel good to be her best friend.

Rosa had spent years as she grew up in Argentina, Papua New Guinea, Beijing, exotic-sounding locations. I was lucky to go as far as the Central Coast an hour out of Sydney for a day. Despite or because of her international accentless voice she couldn't settle. She wasn't easily accepted in Australia.

Branded (unfairly) as a 'rebel' people in authority seemed to automatically misunderstand her; she got into trouble for doing nothing or people wrongly assuming things about her.

Her parents especially her mother with whom she seemed to be involved in a never-ending argument—from when she got up to when she went to bed, that is if she went to bed. Instead likely sneaking out to music bars at nights. And I knew all about that, I stayed at her house often enough.

In the not-rebellion, intimacy, sense that we were different, Art Criminals, being with Ray was like being with Roz.

The houses where Rosamond and I lived with our families were close in terms of physical distance, half a kilometre; but socially economically, we lived on different planets. Rosa's family home was a five-bedroom terrace on the high ground of Blackwattle Ridge. After Aphrodite finished renovations Rosa frequently said she disliked the new Palace of Versailles. I wished I had her options of refusal instead of mine. The house where father, grandfather and I lived together was a rundown never-to-be renovated half-a-cottage, near a pub.

At night I would lie awake, prevented from sleeping by sounds from outside, monologues of strange wanderers that congregated under the street-light behind our tiny back yard.

The music of sleepless nights is imprinted on my soul. At the most unexpected of times, it creeps into mind and plays through my dreams, a hidden undercurrent I'd like to be able to celebrate but I can't; it still hurts too much. I lay huddled, cold in winter, hot in summer; wishing mother were alive to read me a story from a fairy tale book I still remember, even though I must have been only three years old.

I heard swooping unintelligible threats and howls.
'Geroutof there, you bitch—'
Scary staccato shouts—'Hey, Princess!!'
'Words of abuse'—The berating of bitterness and grief.
'You bastard, why did you do it, why did you fucken do it?'

Untitled #11

Untitled #12

Bellows of frustration, screeching insane laughter.

A woman's voice swooping, slurring, sliding, and falling—
Deep dark music. Swirling undercurrents forever through my memory. A music I knew deeply more closely than I knew Bach the musical master whom grandpa played endlessly as if spinning a sonic cocoon to block out the world outside.

Always Bach.

'Listen Margarita. Bach is the master of the art of fugue form. Listen.

The subject inverted, distorted, repeated and embellished; the voices chasing, circularity, and in the melody again—here it comes, now! The subject finds itself in another version, transformed.'

In the daytimes, I listened to father's favourite, Bach's *Art of Fugue*. At night, heard sounds of the wounded, damaged. Jagged fragments—breaking glass, shouts—cutting the night.

Sometimes I heard warm voices talking excitement woven into the night-noise, drowned out by the louder voices.

I was scared of the voices of sadness, desolation, despair; voices of hopelessness and hatred, voices of people taken to drink and drugs to ease untold agony, and which as they are unable to stop their pain turn in fights that made me sweat with fear.

—A man's rough shout, a woman's frightened squeal—A struggle, a fight—Her voice shrilling—His voice—Bitch—kiss me, kiss me—Thumping—cracking fence breaking—A woman sobbing—hard running—broken footsteps trailing away...

I cried that night terrified of what was happening outside, what might happen if I found myself caught out alone at night.

That was how it was before I grew up. Learned how to put on make-up, swear, hold my own. Met Rosamond.

If I heard the backstreet nocturnes when I was a teenager, the dark night music, I swore, put a pillow over my head, told myself they were losers. Why did they not make something constructive of their lives? Life is a gift; if you waste it, you'll be unhappy, I thought. I was never going to do that.

We went out to live music bars. Roz leading the way, but needing me with her to lend my support. I was her sidekick; I found that out pretty quickly. But I wasn't going to let myself be treated like a second fiddle without getting my own back. And I did. It used to give me a secret kick to test her, tease her (which I never let her know). I'd say 'I'm tired, why don't you go out alone, Roz?' Or, even crueller, I'd suggest leaving her, alone.

'I'm going, Roz, it's boring.'

Her reaction, affection underscored by panic, as she squeezed my hand, put her arm around me, intimacy.

'What?"

'Surely you jest!!' Becoming anxious. 'Don't go Margy, you must stay, you have to—It's no fun when you're not here.' Then, 'please stay Margy PLEASE! I beg you, don't leave me! You can't leave me this way.' Sulking and pouting acting as if she was desperate.

'Margy please! Pretty please. I'll let you wear my purple flares, white platforms, red dress! I'll bring you breakfast in bed!' That would do it. After letting her grovel, I gave in.

Rosa was looking for some cool good-looking musician or artist to fall in love with and bore me silly about. She started, a fact of life she practically inscribed on a badge, she made me so aware of it with her knowing ways, self-satisfied smile, distance like a chasm, a gulf war, a boyfriend.

Yes, the years in Adelaide with Ray were fun, triumphant, dripping with the smell of his patchouli. Salty with art-rage. I studied violin at the Conservatorium. I was in love with my violin. I had no regrets.

'All's fair in love and war' was the expression Rosa used to use—delivered with a smile and a toss of her long auburn hair. Now I was the one with the chance to say it, and say it I did, often, to Ray, in those first days overlooking the ocean, in the apartment house above the bait and tackle shop; the flat which Rosa found for herself and Ray, which she had talked about as if it were some kind of *auto da fe*.

I could never get what she was raving about. I couldn't wait 'til Ray and I got out of there. It was much too small.

One by one all Ray's friends, his 'partners in art and crime', shifted to Sydney. And then we did the trek ourselves. Packed our bags, hitched a ride in a Mack truck. Two days and nights later banged on John-Boy's door in a street of Newtown, out of breath, laughing, high on adventure. It took only a couple of months before Ray began to slide in a trajectory of negation destruction that I couldn't, wouldn't, begin to follow him on. For me, moving to Sydney was returning home. For Ray it was like a chance to play multiple roles in a Hieronymus Bosch *Garden of Earthly Delights* horror video. Doing heroin with John-Boy. Kings Cross, with who? I would wonder, sleepless, fearful, in the cottage, waiting for him to return, days later, spattered in blood and vomit, needle marks in his arms, eyes black holes in his head, lipstick smeared all over his body. It was terrifying.

The Cross attracted him to its poisoned heart, like a corpse to a starving dog that can't avoid toxicity. He was fascinated by decomposition. The shapes that humans make as they fall. The flash of steel as it slides through skin, the dizzy rush of blood as it hits brain. His artworks reflected obsessions. The 'Dissection Suite.' Photographic shots of a rabbit pinned, superimposed onto the back of a naked woman. He so tried the lesbian-feminist lecturers at university where he took his degree, after its being withheld due to his final project—self mutilation series; that a term of leave was coined: 'Raymond-leave.'

Just one bullet-point fact on the list from the X-Ray Files. I found out by chance on running into one of his ex-lecturers, Cherie, in Elyssianne's after I left after all the wasted years—and took to unwinding there.

When I told Cherie I'd been in a relationship with Ray, she almost fell off her barstool. I felt I had to buy her a drink to help her recover and then she recounted tale after tale of his depravities, which were not, unfortunately, news to me.

Prostitutes, junkies. Ray fell in love with the chimeras of the Cross underworld, at first returning to be bandaged up by Nurse Marg. And later as decline kicked in, to try to drag her down to his level. His niche in Dante's vision of Hell.

It's strange that I still find it easier to talk about his abuse in third person, describe it in metaphor, or in terms of other people. I find it hard to believe 'domestic violence' happened to me although whether or not he, the 'real Raymond'—and I always believed that beneath the bubbling cauldron polluting his mind he still was there to be found—was responsible or whether it was the drugs or alcohol, or a combination—Ray-from-Hell, Hell-Raiser, Hell's Razor—whether it makes any difference, whether I should feel sorry for him, I don't know.

He went through rehab and he changed. It seems that it was because of drugs that he was violent, aggressive; I am not cutting him out of my life altogether, at least not yet.

Which perhaps is the reason why he still keeps leaning on the bell at strange night hours, pleading through the intercom to be allowed in from the guilt of the remorse playing in his head. And why I do let him in to sleep on the living room floor. It has made problems with girlfriends. But I don't want to feel responsible if Ray jumps off the Harbour Bridge if I don't open the door.

Rosamond's disappearance was bad enough.

I don't want Raymond's death. I don't want him to die.

I visit grandfather. He is ailing now, but able to live alone.

He brings out the records, places one on the old turntable.

Airs of fugue drift quivering through the musty room, the searing clean profound beauty of a violin. Viola. Cello.

'Ah,' he leans against a tapestry antimacassar on the back of his armchair. 'The hart in the wood' stitched by my mother as a girl, long ago, in another country.

His eyes close.

Desert Ruby

Ruby

David Yorricks Gallery, 14 December 2001

'*Rosa.*' His voice was the same, a breathy tenor. 'Ray.' I replied, he was staring at me in bemusement.

Then, 'Rosa?' I asked.

Rosa. Rosa, it was very familiar.

'Rosa. Rosamond. Where have you been?'

'What are you doing here?' I asked, as if the last time I'd seen him was two weeks ago.

'I'm here to see the art,' he said. 'What about you?'

'Likewise.'

'My name's Ruby,' I add, but he doesn't seem to register it. Behind him, the open door, the Australian night.

'I can't hear you, it's noisy, let's go outside, Rosa,' he said.

It happened fast then. I followed him out the door. Bang! We were back where we'd left off. As if the years hadn't passed. Maybe it wasn't ten years.

At least, I tried to think that. But Ray was bigger. His skin redder, dry, coarsened. His eyes I remembered as pale blue, visionary, behind glasses that were often held together with tape, were peering at me through designer frames. His once cropped red hair longer, sticking out in odd looking tufty clumps.

'Come back to my place if you like,' he said. 'For a drink.'

'Okay.'

We walked through the night air of half familiar streets, as if feeling the way forward. The past was behind us, an ocean separating continents. I wasn't sure if I had finished crossing it. I didn't know if I'd landed on a friendly beach or if I was still in a boat on an unknown sea. He walked towards an old car.

'I parked here to avoid the junkies,' he said with a laugh.

I must have looked surprised.

'This car has been broken into,' he assured me.

'They'd break into anything, junkies.' He laughed. I looked apprehensively at bins in the laneway we were walking down. He saw my look and laughed again.

As if there could be a junkie waiting inside to jump out! I pulled my shawl tightly around my shoulders. I'd never gone near heroin. Nor had anything to do with junkies.

Ray walked to the driver's side. He climbed in, unlocked the passenger door from the inside. Hugo held the door open for me. This was different, better, natural, I thought. I ducked my head; he flung armfuls of papers from the passenger seat onto the back seat.

I stepped in and sat down.

'Off to Matraville.' The name was familiar. He unwound the side window winder, rolled down the window. Who really needs air conditioning? I thought.

Ray drove through the heavy traffic. Suddenly I felt faint. I was gasping, trying to breathe in humid heat after crisp cold London air. I looked out the window, feeling dizzy.

The streets looked strangely familiar like a country on a map imagined intensely that you find yourself in.

Like waking from a dream and finding one is holding objects from that dream...

Like waking from a dream and finding one is holding objects from that dream...

Untitled #13

Words from a letter he wrote me long ago rippled through my mind...

I had been here before in cars driving the roads from Surry Hills to Newtown.

We turned into King Street. Ray drove down the long road. I gazed giddily at the strip of restaurants, shops, pubs, theatre, bookshops, clothes stores, furniture shops. Strobe-flickering incandescence, burning my eyes. My hands were shaking.

'How's Margarita?' I forced myself to say.

'Hardly see her. We stopped living together months ago.'

My heart raced. 'Are you living with anyone else?'

'Nope, I'm living my own, that's how I like it.' He cackled.

I started trembling all over as he parked in a dark cul-de-sac. I followed down a narrow pathway overhung with bushes and creepers, towards a cottage.

Hanging on the veranda was a sign. *Alchemy Studios.* Letters punched out of a rectangular metal plate.

'Alchemy Studios,' I said.

'Yep. This is where I live and work.'

'Still trying to find the philosopher's stone?' I said, though I couldn't quite remember the context of the memory.

'Ha, yep that'd be right,' he cackled.

We walked straight into a dark cavernous space.

'Home sweet home,' he turned on the light.

Works in progress on the floor, finished works on walls. I noticed colour studies interspersed with photographic works.

'Can you show me your work?' I asked.

He laughed, and gestured to the walls.

I suddenly remembered what I had found magnetic about his art when we first met in Adelaide.

125

I wrote about his first solo exhibition, it was published in the local paper, before we even became friends.

In the overall body of Ray's work two of the most theoretically and creatively opposed 1970s/early 1980s avant-garde movements came together: colour field and self-mutilation, a combination that I found intriguing, radical and emotionally magnetic. There was nobody else I knew who was doing conceptual visual art that was that self-contradictory. His art works epitomized the buzz word-plaudit of that time: bizarre.

I interpreted his work as being a comment on reason, a legitimate subversion that seemed exciting at that time. Most exciting and gravitational of all was the enigma I saw in his work, a sense of ambiguity and mystery, which left it open to multiple readings, a *tabula rasa* for my desire for new creative experience and, paradoxically, sensation.

But that was when I first knew him and before anything had happened between us.

I had gone to the opening of Ray's show, *Double Vision*.

A few days later I returned. Restlessly prowled between the walls of his work. As I walked, I caught flashes of my reflection in the windows and the glass on the prints on the walls, the endlessly recurring optical patterns, pathways, possibilities; letting me into an altered state of reality, a new colour field of vision. The feeling of excitement it gave me was like the illusion of finding a new colour that only he and I could see.

Now I looked around at the curious assortment of objects, which did not seem to bear much relation to the works on the walls. At least not to the colour studies.

Dissecting bottles, bell jars. Taxidermy birds lined shelves

A snow-dome in a fireplace surrounded by plastic toys, kitsch objects. Collections of signs. It looked almost identical to the studios he worked in when we were living together. As if the room were an exhibit of itself. In Remembrance of Things Past. A set in which we were the fumbling actors.

'Are you still making colour studies?'

'No, I haven't for years. I've been doing photographic and digital works. My last exhibition used a method of photography using a pinhole camera. Here,' he gestured to a wall.

Images of a beach in hypnotically heavy shades of green. I had an image of walking through trees, hypnotic humidity, it was suffocating, how it eased as I walked out of the rainforest.

He started to tell me about how to use a pinhole camera, and how he made these images. It was hard to concentrate on his photographs with all the dead things in jars under them.

I was relieved when he offered beer. An escape route (even though usually I don't drink it). The further away I was from formaldehyde at that moment the better. We sat on a recycled car seat in front of pickled things. On the eighth or ninth or tenth bottle that we shared, he staggered over, kissed me.

'Let's lie down,' he said after a while.

'My sleeping quarters are this way.'

He took my hand. I followed him to a ladder in the corner, which led up to a mezzanine that held a bed.

'This is the cubby,' he said. 'I built it myself.'

It was different. Not to issue commands. Not to attempt to verbalise nuances of desire into elaborate codified artifice of ritual theatre. Not to put on a costume drama and role play the Ideal Woman in infinite variations. Cleopatra, Boadicea, Venus.

To just be natural, be myself.

Ruby Love.

Afterwards, neither of us could sleep.

'What are you doing with your art?' I asked.

'Just pushing buttons. Trying to find something rare. I'm leaving for the desert tomorrow. Leaving at 11.30 a.m.. Flying in a biplane. There's an opal-mining town on the edge of desert in South Australia. Blokes leave their families, sink savings into opal mines for twenty years hoping to make their fortune. They live in caves they dig from rock because it's too hot above ground.'

'Coober Pedy. I've been there. Before I met you. When I was travelling. Did you say you were flying there?'

'Yeah, with a mate of mine, Bob. He's a flying instructor. I'm learning to fly. I've almost got my pilot's license. Just need to do another twenty flying hours. I'm going to stay there five days while Bob does courier work.... Then he's returning to Coober Pedy and I'm going to fly back to Sydney. Should be a blast, baby, a real blast.'

I turned and looked at him with narrowed eyes. Ray, the Red Baron.

'Can I come with you?'

'You want to?' He laughed. 'What about what's-his-face?'

'Hugo?' I reached for his cigarette. I took a drag and blew a steady plume of smoke above our faces.

'Hugo's history.'

TIN SHED CAMP SITE
Coober Pedy, 15 December, 2001

We all fall down. Going down. When he falls down I fall under, sucked into succulent waving clouds of bliss that funnel into cyclone dark suction clouds that fog my eyes, suck me down. I think it will be into him but then I find myself alone on a dark plain, the cyclone man has disappeared sucked me in with sweet-seduction lines, a low tone spun me round with wild abandon, addictive as necessity, left me on a lonely plain and blasted off somewhere else.

I'm in a desert. Wind is howling. Stunted bushes ripped up from the dusty ground, uprooted flung into the sky. Where am I? In a howling night, in the middle of the howling storm?

I wake up; walls and roof of the tin shed rattle and shake as if about to be blown away. The wind is screeching outside. Aboriginal spirits furious we are here, foreigners who do not know their names, cannot recognise them. Suddenly terrified, I turn, reach for Ray. My hand feels across the bed. My fingertips touch the shaking tin. He's not there.

I sit up, struggling to breathe. There should be a torch by the bed; my hands fumble in darkness. I'm filled with horror, spinning thoughts of ghosts and spirits. What is going on?

My hand locates the metallic barrel of the torch, I push the switch and a beam of thin light extends before me, lighting up a stripe of the hut.

My God, what's that? Crouched against the far wall of the hut is... A hideously deformed shape, colours of flesh and blood, wrenchingly familiar in shape, but there's something wrong, curled into itself, deformed bud; it's grotesque, sad.

When I had unknowingly conceived I had a dream, a nightmare, of a baby with no head sitting on a bed. That's what's before my eyes now. A foetus with no head is here in the hut. O God. It's like one of those nightmares where you open your mouth but the scream freezes inside your head. Panicking on swirling waves of fear. I'm caught in the suspended silence, terror, gap of a frozen scream. There's nothing to hold onto. No talisman, nor rock of comfort, no person. My fingernails gouge into the flesh of my hands, I bite my lip.

I force myself to look, as I do the vision disappears. Transforms into Ray's backpack, filled with painting things, flung carelessly into a corner of the tin-hut. An after-image lingers on dark air. The foetus. Ray's baby. Never talked of between us. One of the many things not talked about between us. My baby. The baby deformed, never existed, never viable. What was it doing in this hut, in my head?

The tin-hut rattling and shaking, tin can bouncing down a street kicked by a careless schoolgirl from Kansas. At least she had a little dog. I've never had a little dog. Where is Ray? I shine torchlight around the hut. Don't see any more phantoms. One is enough. His shirt is missing from the hook on the door. I decide I had better get up and see if I can find him. But there seems to be a strange relation developing between me and my thoughts as if there's my consciousness, shining lamp, a bulb, a pearl of illumination, and then there's a long jagged unravelling string of a balloon connecting my little glow of consciousness to thoughts which fly high and almost free like balloons on the end of the strings above my head. A bunch of balloons in the hand of an old balloon seller in my picture book from childhood. A funfair balloon in my child's hand, there's been no other child in my life. Only me.

I stand up unsteadily, swing in a sweeping arc towards the door. I reach up feeling like a princess, a goddess, swinging in an arc of perfection; the hook is crawling with ants.

Then I stroll, I bowl, open the tin-hut door into the gusting night. Opening the door like a mouth opening to laugh and laughter is the wind ripping through the tin-hut shanty-town of the campsite, like the life of the party.

Ray is nowhere in sight.

But then I look up.

And I see him.

Raymond and Margarita—and me…

The images airbrushed, gorgeous, like balloons floating in the sky, suspended in not quite lifelike technicolour on the screen of the drive-in that towers above the campsite like a message from god, or an alien visitation. I lean against a shaking corrugated iron wall and turn my eyes to heaven, images projected into the sky. Then it all changes.

I am shocked to see a pornographic movie. The drive-in has been showing them. I don't want to watch.

Going down, falling down, into unconsciousness.

Next morning, I am sipping mineral water and brushing dust from my hair, in the tin shed. Ray laughs.

'I thought you liked drugs. It was a surprise, a gift. LSD to make Mr Leary's eyes pop.'

'What gave you that idea? I like drugs when I know and if I choose Ray, and often not then.' I say weakly glancing up at the blank screen of the drive-in hovering above us.

'I never want to take another drug in my life.'

'Ooh-Ooh,' Ray makes goo-goo baby eyes.

131

Untitled #14

...falling down, into unconsciousness.

The headless foetus flashes in my mind. Last night is not one I will want to remember. Apparently Ray went for a walk in the wind-storm. He found me on his return slumped on the iron-hard ground outside the hut and carried me into the hut, to bed.

I walk outside. Look away from the campsite. The endless horizon surrounds the desert in an enclosure more profound than any fences. My mind swirls, balloons bobbing above my head, reaching for the freedom of eternity, the sky.

I think. Does the future have any less reality than the past or does it hold more reality, as it's going to happen, it's coming. A foreshadow heavy and full with immanence whereas the past is gone; it remains in past shadows, memories, causes rather than effects? What has more reality, cause or effect? And if it's effect, is Future effect or tiny beams of a moment slicing a scythe, grim reaper's sickle, through the seething mass of Time—action, events, and matter, space— we call 'reality'? Is the present moment an effect, and if so, how many effects make up that moment?

And if we take this model of reality, of Time to be true, how do we account for 'facts' that so many worlds are sealed off, separated from us, by Time; they exist in a different time to us. A different time and different space. The farther away in space, is the farther away in time; but I can travel through Time, Space, in thoughts, dreams, in space probe missions; I can watch images beamed from Mars, the Moon, images, five thousand years ago in our past, but we can see them from our vantage point here in our present.

We are not there; we are here, on Earth, light years away. We can see images from 'there', so far removed they are objects of curiosity, wonder, dream only. Like sacred objects, or fetishes of a tribe.

I am in the present now but feel that I am also in another world, observing, recording another dimension of existence. The Past. Planet Raymond. I'm in the space cart on a space mission. In my mind filming everything around me as it happens. But it's light years away, a life away, a thousand years away from my present life.

That's what I think then I remember I'm not at home now with Hugo curled up in front of the TV screen watching images transmitted from a red planet with green sky. Watching the cart lumber over to investigate Martian rock. I am in the space-cart, driving the vehicle, operating the controls and the camera. This is reality. I am here.

Stepping out from a space vehicle onto the red earth.

I look up and above me is the green sky.

I exist beyond boundaries limits, in the mirage shimmer, in illusory ripples, riding, tightening and shaking the air.

Waterless waves on the invisible long-lost ocean.

All that exists, left from the ancient inland sea is a massive expanse of sand pan and rock like images of the surface of planet Mars beamed down from the Pathfinder onto campsite TV screens. In yesterday's newspaper I read an article by an astrophysicist who wrote we do not need to go to Mars to find out what Time does. We can find out right here in Australia, in the ancient life forms. Here in this landscape of endlessness are the natural scenarios to test why oceans dry up and disappear.

In Australia as on Mars, it's already happened, a very long time ago.

The catastrophe, of nature, struck and what exists now is

the parched future of an ancient inland sea.

Find out from the landscape, as you find out from the art about human nature, if you know how to read the signs. Lie on my back on the red earth, and screw up my eyes against the sky. Tears like rivers rush down the sides of my face.

How many perished trying to find that mirage? Hoping to find a freshwater lake teeming with life. And arrived here, in the desert, illusory wilderness of illusions, a million years or two, too late.

But then there is Kati Thanda. Too salty to drink, someone found, ephemeral pink lake, disappearing Kati Thanda-Lake Eyre emerges at random times throughout the century, and covers hundreds of kilometres. The water flattens at midday. Into a reflective surface, a mirror sky, reflected in the lake so sailors can't tell which is sky and which is lake, you're sailing in the sky if you're in a yacht.

I read about it before everything went psychedelic.

Ruby sailing in a pink lake in the sky.

Ruby in the pink sky sailing.

Ruby in the sky with opals.

I wake with dust in my eyes and hair filled with red dust. The corrugated iron wall-rattle shakes my bones like a wake-up call from a splintering noisy past I'm trying to box-up and present as a gift for the morning, the feeling of everything's all right that would please Hugo in Rivers Chase our Primrose Hill house. Lasting so long out here in the endless lost highway mirage-ripple-refracting-hallucination.

What's important and maybe all that counts now is that I am real, myself.

Raymond's tousled red hair, his face, sleeping on the pillow, and I still see Margarita. See her bigger than the drive-in screen over this tin-hut site like Big Brother's spy-eye forever spying on us looming over us even in the desert.

I see my closest friend, laughing caught forever in headlights. Drive-in screams. Margarita playing violin, laughing so in Ronny's Green Room, playing pool, play the one they want to have, sweetest luscious delicious plump sweet-fleshed Margarita.

But what am I thinking, I am, past, thinking, of what-am-I thinking of, doing, living in the present moment of pure psychic derangement, blowing, screeching grains of bull-dust, red thick sticky matting reddened hair, maddening as bees in swarm; heat, shimmers, coalesces white-slide white-hide white-blast white-radiation-blaze white-fear ripples black and white.

I get up free—I say—I turn, and say to Ray—wake up baby we're here—in the middle of the desert, baby, you and me—and words stick in my throat like the shape of stranded travellers I have heard of who lie down in the middle of the highway run over by road-train trucks. A crescent, like a kind of smile, curled up, embryonic, grin-grim reality of foetal attraction. The truck drivers simply cannot see them in mirage ripples of heat on the roads. They curl up and they die.

I shake Ray, try to wake him; I observe the outside husk of Ray like a planet, non-responsive exterior of his sleeping skin. Where are you? When I need you?

But I can't stir him. It's as if he really is dead. Lost within his skin. I want to catch his Rapid Eye Movements with whispers of my tongue but I know it's hopeless. I shall have to go alone, go it alone.

When I push open the door of the hut, the glare hits my eyes like onslaught of migraine—flashing lights, ringing bells—trembling, blurry, flicker—mirage-whirl like how I imagine an epileptic fit might start

Black-white—black-white—the zig—the zagzig interior-exterior to

Sharp as a knife underside—shimmering—reality—daze--rays like water—all looks like water out there

I rub my eyes and colours run and run—like tears—blurring merging refracting, rainbow-resonance-sad children lost forever in the endless desert—that stretches around us—like a mother nature forgotten how to nurture.

All she wants to do is peel off the seven veils and dissemble, dance and drift, nature disaffected, blown away.

All we can do now is look after each other.

But we've forgotten how to do that.

I think of opal miners in stony heat blasted plots turning to dust in burning heat of hope, I shudder, I hear her.

Margy calling from faraway. The high-pitched notes of violin solos soaring through glistening sky on fire with light, heat, illusions of water—dripping slippery-slide into eyes—elemental vessel boat of the soul. Physical. Bodily. Generative. Re-generative.

Not one. But many, multiplied, multiple, baby, got boxed, got out of my box.

—Shimmering ripple wave— Unfolding—fold (unfold) all around me—Deep inside of me is you—

I walk away from the campsite towards the town to find I set off hoping to find cappuccino, or latte, espresso, flat white, short black, long black, would do.

Although trying to forget it, the vista of rippling illusions and mirages is not easily dismissed. Head down, to the hard ground. Grounding.

Sun-blasted surface beneath which who knows how many unseen opals lie in darkness, to await the miner, and polished, revealed, discovered, appreciated as gemstones. I saw them in shops in the Rocks where Hugo and I had browsed absorbed as any tourists in the treasures of the tourist economy.

WILD WEST SHOOT OUT!!
GUN FIGHT IN COOBER MAIN STREET!

As I walk down the main street I pass supermarket windows, covered with faded news articles on gunfights in Main Street.

At the newsagent there is a new headline.

LONDON ART DEALER DISAPPEARS!

The words jump off the sandwich board.

Reaching Tilly's Treasure Trove, cave café, keeping an eye out for gunslingers. And lone deranger art dealers.

Here in this cavern with no windows seems almost as hip as inner city London basement taverns, because it's so surreal. And then it starts.

Deck the Halls with Boughs of Holly/All through the Night...

A waitress approaches. Dressed in pink-and-white check overall, smiling scarily, blonde hair, eyes bright blue. I expect her to hand the menu carved on steak a bad-taste joke for a hangover mouth, but no, it's the usual plastic laminate list of focaccia and bagels and coffee.

'A flat white, please,' I say.

'Sugar?'

'Sugar? Um. No thanks.'

When I was studying—

When I first met Hugo—

I loved pre-Socratic philosophers, whose ideas are passed on as fragments only, like poetry of Sappho of the ancient world.

Raw voices, first voices, strange freshness of ancient voices speaking down through centuries, in a profound and brilliant poetry, sense beyond sense. I found a book in Ray's place and brought it with me.

Lying in a tin-hut in the desert, in the middle of opal fields, lying on my back on the narrow bed on a sheet that is red with throat-catching dust, door open.

The furnace-hot water colours of the watercolour world shimmer. This is what I see: a slice of wooden campsite fence, above it looming white screen of the drive-in flanked by ochre red of land, blue of the sky, so light it's blue-white, rippling and shaking as if it were water, it's impossible not to smile at the unreality of it, like lying in the middle of a hallucination, but no it's like flying in a landscape as it's painted; a world in formation, the unstable world of a shimmering ancient phase before it settles into solid material form, fluid, intangible and untouchable—before the colours dry.

I want to merge with those waves and tremors, I want to lose myself in the haze of unreality, disappear in the illusion of water in heat: dissolve my spirit in the spirit of this an-cient land, the country which is neither state of being nor of nothingness, in a state of non-being metamorphosing in the dreaming spirit and living forever in the mind of an ancient race. I take out a book. Open it at random.

Pre-Socratics...43...52...63...71...82, eyes slide down the numbered sections and take a hold...

The words and letters run together dance off the page before my eyes to the shimmering veil waving moistly, seductively.

Once again the land is doing its dance of the seven veils, stripping off certainties, securities, layer by layer... first to go is the perception of solidity, the tangible substance of matter, the belief that it holds its shape goes in sweetly joyous ripples; next the perception of distance, the comforting security of a horizon to put a boundary, limit, on one's view of the world— that goes with a belly-roll of infinite space; buzz of flies, stench of rotten flesh decomposing by the side of a road that stretches a ribbon life-line, and road kill death-line, across desert tracks invisible to the untrained physical eye; earth blown away, rock reduced to sand, dust, layer by layer, the surface shifts and slides blown away by the wind.

I imagine streets blown away in the night, city parks erod-ed, tower blocks rippling in a haze and disappearing, the Gallery, our house in Primrose Hill, shaking and sliding into a puddle of heat, they were never really there at all...

I think of Hugo in his olive-green three-piece suit, glass of burgundy in hand, beaming at me with a cheery twinkle; and now Hugo is rippling and shimmering, Sir Hugo, sliding slip-ping, growing long and thin, fat; dear Hugo is doing a dance of seven veils blowing me a kiss, Hugo is holding out his arms entreatingly, Hugo is disappearing, now I see all along it was a mirage—which I couldn't see. Come back I call, too late.

It's all blown away like sand by the wind at night revealed as illusory-insubstantial—colours floating across a void.

I hear an approach. Feel footsteps reverberating through dry ground. Tin walls rattling.

The door pushes open, and I look in shock. He is standing in the doorway, enlarged by the small shed, tee-shirt and shorts covered in layers of red dust, reddening further his hair that sticks out around his head as if he's a cartoon character, eyes pale as the sky and as distant behind glasses. I catch all this in a split-second, like a swimmer in trouble sees in a final splashing upsurge a longed-for shore.

'Did you do any drawing?' Encouraging was my wont.

'I went and had a coffee at the cafe on the main street next to the supermarket, the one with all that Wild West shoot-out stuff on the walls. I wrote a letter to Margarita.'

'What?' I am shocked, trying to cover up yet express horror. I am confused, beginning to whirl. I am shaking.

'Margarita?' I didn't know you were still in touch, I mean I didn't know you were still communicating, you told me that you hadn't seen her—You said you weren't together any more.'

He looks at me eyes bemused behind this season's frames. Or am I fooling myself into seeing I've affected him. Furious. Suddenly cold despite the temperature.

'Why are you writing to her?' My voice sounds English, very London. The drug is still affecting me. I will never take another. Of course, I didn't knowingly take it; he forced it upon me unwittingly. He put it into my water. Reprehensible thing to do, I would never have taken it.

He's easing onto the ground, iron-hard earth the floor. He leans back against the wall and springs forward immediately.

'Whoa! Hold on there! That's hot!'

'Well?' I ask again, staring into his glasses, trying to see his eyes if not soul. For I shall know your secrets. And I shall stop at nothing 'til I know.

'We haven't lived together for months, but we still see each other, Roz.' His tone casual. 'Margarita is my best friend. She's done a lot for me, mate.'

The normal social Ray of relationship-speak is not one I'm familiar with. The incongruity momentarily winds me.

After years of dreaming this time through my most intense feelings, it is not 'We' any more in a dreamland vision of golden light. It is two of us in a tin shed in the desert. In the here and now. Separate. Grown up. Autonomous. Individual. Alone.

I hold up my left hand, spread my fingers slowly and stare at my hand, arm stretched out above my head.

Hand of Ruby against tin roof.

Ray's head seen through outstretched fingers of Ruby's left hand.

Margarita always was my best friend. Ray was my lover.

I slowly pull my fingers tight

Twist into a fist I know is pretty.

Ray's head is in his hands. He looks up suddenly.

My eyes connect with his. If you were Hugo, I —This has to stop. What am I thinking of. Hugo is not here. Not here.

I've broken free—to be, my lost and new found identity. Remember everything and myself. O my. It's the heat getting to me.

The heat is pressing like hands of the devil squeezing each of my temples in a vice-grip, devil, but I don't believe in the devil, I've not believed in the devil or evil since I was a kid, at

142

Sunday school in Port Hagen, terrified of the stories of burning in hell, terrified I'd stumble off the track when I grew and lose the grace of childhood innocence that meant all God's children go to Heaven. Made you want to stay a child, innocent, pure, blessed and beloved forever.

I haven't believed in the devil since I stopped believing so what's going on? Primal fear like a spirit, Aboriginal rai, stirs in my bones. A furious fear fills me.

'Let's get out of here. Come on. Let's go into the furnace. Let's eat. I want to see that underground house. See the sights of Coober Pedy!' He stands up. 'Come on: Touristville!!'

'Uh huh'.

There's a sound like beating wings in my ears.

Bats screeching long ago. Dark shadows zooming through purple-black skies. Screeching, shrieking. I jump up, dust puffs out of his jeans which I'm wearing. Clouds of textured red particles rise up making me cough, and fall onto my black leather kitten-heeled shoes. I put on the old straw hat I found at Ray's before we flew in the biplane from Sydney. I follow Ray like a sleepwalker out into the dissolving world.

We are lying on beds in the tin shed. Night-time. Margarita is my best friend. His words loop through my mind.

'Where's Margarita living now?' I ask casually, looking at the bed where he's lying on his back, smoking.

'Ha!' His voice is very loud.

'She's living in a penthouse on George Street. Penthouse death house…'

It sounds as if he's trying to laugh, but instead he coughs, and from the sudden blankness that crosses his face I think it

143

looks like he's in pain.

'Do you have an address or phone number? I'd like to visit her.'

'Yeah. I'll come with you if you're going to see her.'

Margarita

16, The Mayfair, Sunday, 16 December 2001

I am developing a rhythm, living alone. It's been four months now; since I left the Matraville cottage and the turbulent years with Ray. I feel myself slipping into my self-determined life with the 'ah' of deep private satisfaction of sliding into the therapeutic water of a warm fragrant bath. Feels like letting go. It feels good. I still hear cicadas. But that does not bother me. I am developing strategies for dealing with my anxieties.

Like now, lying on the Sir Hugo velvet couch propped on green cashmere cushions as the haunting first bars of Bach's *Art of Fugue* drift through still warm air. I stripped out of my work clothes as soon as I got home. Slipped off shoes. Wriggled out off black skirt, peeled off sky-blue silk blouse. Rolled down tights, uncovering smooth skin of my legs. I admire the anklet tattoo on my left ankle.

I leave my silk tights on the floorboards. I am naked alone in someone else's lavish apartment (he is away and has let me stay). The sensation of bare soles on polished boards is delicious as paddling after months of heels. I look at my photographs on the wall. Images of Rosamond at the Farm, one summertime, I have arranged my prints around a painting that Ray gave me, the year everything changed.

He brought a gift when I was alone in the apartment in the

rooming house we called the Haunted Castle. That was such a surprise. There had been a knocking on the door.

'Who is it?' I had called cautiously.

'It's Raymond'. My heart sped. Something was wrong.

'What's happened?' I opened the door, worried that Rosa was in trouble or hurt.

And there he was. Blue shorts, straw hat. Bottle of wine in one hand and colour study in the other, smiling. The smell of perspiration mingled with his patchouli oil.

'G'day!' He was smiling broadly. 'Thought I'd visit you. See if you're okay, what with all the drunks around here.'

I'd been practicing, and was holding my violin.

'Come in.' I said.

He asked me to, and so I played him my audition piece for the Conservatorium. Bach's fugues from Contrapunctus 1 to 4.

I interpreted as the soprano 'voice' in each of these simple fugues in the *Art of Fugue*, and played them as a soloist.

Then I opened the wine and we drank the bottle.

I don't remember all we talked about. Art and music. And Rosa. I remember he said she was hard to live with. She didn't eat, let alone cook. Writing, painting. That's all she did. I sympathised. I was surprised, delighted that he had decided to confide. I wasn't happy with Rosa then, not after she had moved out from our flat and into a flat with him. And it was like a gift to have him visit me, alone. Someone to talk to who seemed to care about me in the Castle.

Talk, and that's all we did. On his first visit.

I walk into the bathroom, and look in the mirror. A black haired woman of indeterminate age stares back. In the years of Rosamond I used to think I was ugly. It's taken a long time to see myself as attractive. Black hair frames my pale heart-shaped face, curling over my shoulders to breasts. I'm plump, yes, but so? I've grown to like my plump thighs, belly, softness of my chin. It's only when I am with others that I become can become self-conscious. Ray didn't mind my body at first. 'I like tummy,' he said, 'I don't like anorexic women.' But later in the last years he mocked me as much for my curves as my violin. Before I moved out.

I sweep my long black curly hair away from my face; gaze at my sky blue eyes, which I inherited from my mother. 'Irish eyes,' Rosamond used to say. It's ridiculous. I can't even look at myself in a mirror without thinking of Ray and Rosa, how they viewed me. It's as if they're hiding within me, they've become deeply part of 'me,' my sense of self, the image I have of myself, and I'll never escape their gaze. That's inside me.

Then I hear cicada. That familiar shriek powering up drilling into my ears. Like a workman's drill from outside in the endless reconstructions. As if all that's done to reconstruct this worked-over city cannot be enough. Sydney is a property developer's wife addicted to surgery; the more blankly 'perfected' she looks, the quicker she is subjected to another 'improvement.' Under piles of rubble, holes in the ground, glittering skyscrapers, is a lost Sydney. Even the dead have been moved around.

City of ghosts. The Town Hall just down from this building is built on the site of the Old Sydney Burial Ground that was once where Central railway station is now.[13]

Not long ago, there was excavation work done under the Town Hall, to replace old pipes. The plumbers were shocked to find skeletons, skulls, graves, coffins, funerary relics. Then it came out, that almost a hundred years ago, Devonshire Street Cemetery, the first Old Sydney Burial Ground, was reclaimed to make way for Central Station. Bodies were retrieved from their coffins in the ground and vaults, in states of decay, by their relatives, and were moved to the Town Hall site. But many of the deceased were not able to be moved by their families. They remain buried in the foundations of Central Station, and Town Hall, where there is an underground station.

Untold numbers of the deceased, shadow the living travellers.

I imagine ghosts, shaken by the reverberations of the eternal reconstructions, waiting on lost platforms for ghost trains.

The dead call our names in every way, in every dying day.

Trying to drown the noise of drilling I walk to the compact disc player and put on Bach's *Art of Fugue*, once more.

Glance at photographic images of Rosamond. Angular thin white limbs draped over branches of a ghost gum. The span of hands flung against the sky; sharp arcs of shoulders and hips. We walked to the riverbank and she took off her clothes and lay across the trunk and limbs of the magnificent dead tree.

The humidity presses my skin...where is she?

What happened to Rosa?

Elyssianne's flashes into my thoughts. I went to the club last night. In crowded shadows I saw a familiar face. It's not long since I've been going out but I have a feeling I could become part of the scene.

Images.

Flutter and fall through my mind in a cadence, rose petals, drift through the garden at dusk...Muted colours, grape juice mauve, purple wine stains wine-black tongues.

In a secluded garden, still close air thickens with invisible dark fibres, the velvety enveloping touch of approaching night. Splashing water, a glowing fountain beyond the Fairy Bower's wooden bench where she sits naked. I approach on a pebbled pathway. She's waiting for me, pretending she can't see me, she doesn't want me.

But I know better and
I have ways   I have means
I have kisses
I have a bottle of wine
To convince her in our secret garden game.

She looks up, and rises swiftly, flits down darkening paths. I follow fleeting tantalizing glimpses of ivory-pale skin floating on darkness, she disappears into the arbour. The glow of candlelight appears in the window. I, heart racing, tremble.

She is stretched out on the chaise longue.

Tantalizing, beautiful, cruel.

Indolent, feigning indifference.

In the light of candles glittering in the candelabra on the low table, skin that shone silver in the moonlight is now glowing golden warm as honey...

I walk in after her. Put down offerings, my wine and armful of flowers. And a script, that I wrote and give to her.

The Mystery of the Art of Fugue[14]

The factor X that intrigues musicologists with an interest in Bach's love of gematria, or the number alphabet, was the way Bach was writing his name or, rather, starting to, into the last fugue he was to write in his life, using the number code of his name, which in gematria added up to 14, or 1+4 = 5.

This is the gematria chart:

A= 1   E= 5   I/J= 9   N= 13   R= 17   W= 21
B= 2   F= 6   K= 10   O= 14   S= 18   X= 22
C= 3   G= 7   L= 11   P= 15   T= 19   Y= 23
D= 4   H= 8   M=12   Q= 16   U/V= 20   Z= 24

In gematria BACH equals 14 or 1+4 = 5.

And JS Bach equals 41, which adds up to 5.

Art of Fugue (Die Kunst der Fuge) which, it is claimed, was written to be fully comprehended by reading the music, has fourteen fugues including the last unfinished fugue.

Bach began to write his signature into his fourteenth contrapunctus, at the point that had numerological significance, bar 239 which adds up to 14 (1+4 =5). The fugue breaks off at line 239, and this is where Bach's son wrote on the manuscript that it was at this point that Bach became ill and died. He had a stroke, went blind, and shortly after died.

Bach was, in the last years of his life in Leipzig, a member of Mizler's 'Corresponding Society of the Musical Sciences'. A musical theory discussion society (some say connected to kabbalism) founded by Lorenzo Mizler, a publisher. It was in the eighteenth century, when music, mathematics and philosophy were not yet split up into separate disciplines, and both music and mathematics had esoteric meaning unfamiliar in modern times (though it should be noted that the fugue was a secular form). Mizler sent papers to members who corresponded by letters, he was influenced by rationalist philosopher Gottfried Leibniz, published his papers.

The composers played with what was termed 'puzzle canon' by writing hidden messages using letters of notes (like use of binary digits to represent letters by analogy). Only trained ears, of educated mathematicians, philosophers, composers, scholars assumed, could appreciate the coded messages. (And there are no recorded female composers from that time—however there may have been women and girls in the audiences, for instance Bach's children, amongst them girls who appreciated and knew how to read and likely play music). Bach was writing his signature into his music.

This raises the puzzle that continues to resonate in musicology today. Bach was writing his name into the last fugue, Contrapunctus 14 in the key of B flat in line 239, when he died or 'disappeared' literally and metaphorically. What does this say about the meaning of the message signified by writing his name into the fugue, or starting to?

Some musicologists have drawn parallels with mathematical theory in particular to the logician Gödel's incompleteness theorem. Bach had left notes that suggested he was writing a final fugue for four themes in four voices which would serve as a complex climax to the work as a whole, and there is some speculation that Bach may have left behind somewhere a lost 'fragment X', a page where he worked out the counterpoint between the four subjects.

Whereas such a speculated fragment has never been found, what is known is that Bach was writing his name as the third theme, and there are well founded suggestions that the (perhaps) unwritten 'fourth theme' would have been the melody line that starts the *Art of Fugue* cycle in Contrapunctus 1 and runs throughout the cycle. As Bach was writing himself into his composition, a fugal analogy for the 'death of the author' theory in literature, I suggest, Bach's 'disappearance' self-reflexively illustrates the 'death of the author theory' that authors cannot write what they intend and feel and the 'final' meaning of the text is open to potentially infinite readings/as it is read differently by readers, and 'finished' in various ways by readers and composers. Another way of looking at this is through the lens of mathematician Design, can a designer of systems distance themselves sufficiently from systems to validly test them? Can science effectively test itself, can art break its own rules to self-reflexively step outside of Art?

There are those who say the unfinished fugue is not a valid example of Gödel's incompleteness theorem (let alone death of the author theory), and does not prove anything.

Also, that instead of being able to write him or herself into their 'system' of language, or write something new or 'original' outside it, what such a fugue composer does is create infinite regress, as Bach did in the four mirror fugues he wrote prior to his unfinished fugue Contrapunctus 14. If this were provable it would prove the impossibility of an 'author'/composer bringing something original themselves from outside closed systems of language (created in a 'hierarchical' closed system such as fugue represents) yet this example proves to be a paradox as is much mirroring of self-referentiality, as Bach did literally disappear as he wrote himself into his fugue, this was a break from and in his 'system'. What is most profound is that Bach's unfinished fugue 'writes' its author's absence, the disappearance of the writing subject. This may have meaning, presence on a reflexive frequency that we can't apprehend in the 'material/spiritual' way in the division of body/mind, life and death; that occurs in this fugue music.

However it is symbolically and literally extraordinary that Bach 'disappeared' as he wrote his own name into his composition (his fugue system). Perhaps the mythical lost 'fragment X' is author-God of the 'system'. A full performance of Bach's

Art of Fugue was not possible in his time scholars believe, due to its complexity. The collection of counterpoint works in the *Art of Fugue* was written to be read and understood, as Bach may have seen it 'in the mind of God'. Or, author-God. Or, reader-God (nowadays Author-Publisher? Artist Designer?).

It was a collection Bach wrote for teaching fugue.

What is the deep relation of music to the instrument, the mind and bodies' feelings to created text? To what extent can a composer write herself into their works? To what extent is a composition the author's? Can a text kill, or absorb, devour its author? Can a composer write him or her self into another reality, an after-life? And what would that mean?

That is the crux of the unanswerable question.

And there is another question I have, musical instruments were used in the sixteen-hundreds to connect with the divine, they were tools to reach a higher level of knowledge, through applying mathematics in music. Nowadays can writing tools, computers, help us to find where we come from?   MM

And I have a bottle of wine. I rush to her, kneel beside her. She stares at me and looks away.

Something else is needed in this perfect scenario. To bring it alive, make her mine...I find the corkscrew under the chaise longue. Uncork the wine and pour it into goblets.

Raising hands in solemn toast, we drink deeply.

I am transfixed. Her lips so near.

I lean towards her, touch her, slide my hands behind her neck and pull her face, her lips towards mine. I kiss her gently at first, and then—

—A bell rings, she jumps up, a stricken look on her face. She rushes out the door into the garden through which I find as I hastily attempt to follow a westerly gale is blowing from the deserts hundreds of kilometres inland. The burning wind pulls my hair, pushes me back; I cannot see where I am going or where she has gone.

And she is gone.

Lost in Newcastle

Hugo

Sydney-Newcastle train, 17 December, 2001

I caught the train at Central at 7.35 a.m.. By the time I left the hotel it was hot. Maybe it was the humidity, climate, or anxiety. The skin on my hands and lower arms was itchy, red and blistering into eczema, which I suffered as a boy, and which had not afflicted me since until now, uncomfortably, with my arm. Every movement made me want to scratch.

Apart from scratching, all I could think of was Ruby and the conversation I had the previous afternoon by phone with a young man, Alex Robinson, who may or may not be Ruby's brother, whom I was travelling north to meet. I thought it unlikely, he said his missing sister was called Rosamond, Roz for short. It's a charming name but not my Ruby. Still I am following the lead. He seemed convinced, and his stated identifying physical feature I confirmed. A very slight abnormality of a left ear lobe. Given Ruby's previous amnesia it could eventuate.

I will follow all reasonable links.

I did not stop at a chemist to purchase anti-itching unguent; I might have missed the train. I didn't risk looking for a pharmacy but instead boarded the train scratching surreptitiously at bloody sores on backs of my hands, peeling shreds between fingers. Along with my Wittgenstein, and Kant, I had a bottle of beer with me, and a pack of cigarettes purchased at

Sydney airport for our stay in Sydney.

But the moment I lit up with a grateful sigh, before the train left I was accosted by a shrieking woman with long dark hair, in a kaftan dress, who shot up out of the row of seats in front of me, like some furious puppet-show Judy, demanding to know if I could read.

'Yes, my dear,' I replied evenly. 'I can read and also write.'

'Well, what does that say?' Stabbing the forefinger of her hand at a sign that, as I peered without my glasses, I did notice now at the far end of the carriage, just below the ceiling.

'No Smoking.' I laughed weakly, as much as I was capable of laughing in the circumstances.

If she were not so energetically domineering, I would not have been able to raise a smile. An image of Ruby whipped my conscience into an instant agony of remorse. I stabbed out the cigarette on the heel of my brogue; and itching, scratching, set off to find the smoking carriage.

Every carriage displayed the No Smoking sign of the times. Health Fascists have wasted no time in Australia I thought as the train took off and I located a uniformed guard.

'I'm looking for the Smoker's carriage,' I said.

'Sorry sir, no smoking on Spirit of Progress.'

'What about drinking? In the Spirit of Progress?'

'You may purchase alcoholic beverages in the buffet with meals.

The buffet opens in approximately ten minutes time, sir.'

'Yes, yes. Thank you.'

Where could she be? Ruby. I couldn't wait, walked through two carriages and found the buffet to purchase the first scotch of the journey. My growing anxiety submerged the interest I would otherwise have reserved for scenery, my thoughts and emotions removed, detached from the view. Still, I gazed, as if hoping to find answers in this strange land. Where are you? The train traversed a bridge over the Hawkesbury River. I had remarked upon it to Ruby when studying maps in the hotel.

The view was indeed spectacular, but I couldn't focus on it. The train skirted a vast expanse of water, an inlet of the sea. Around this, wooded hillsides sloped at steep angles against the sky; I could see exposed oyster beds, on the far side houses, on the edge of the water that looked to be only accessible by boat.

I pictured her in a boat, my lost Lady of Shalott. I scratched my wrists and gazed up into that foreign blue and opened a miniature bottle of scotch, and for the first time since my gall bladder operation, wished I believed in a God I could pray to.

Alex

Fern Cottage, Rose Street, Adamstown

It was me who saw the pictures first and recognized Roz. For days her face has been on TV and over the newspapers, but even so, I don't know if Aphrodite would have recognized her if I hadn't told her, even then I had to insist that it was. When I first heard it was on the radio. 'London Art Dealer Disappears at Sydney Opening', or words to that effect. I was working on my old mountain bike, getting ready for the Cyclops Trials. Changing the bearings and oiling the brake cables. I thought it sounded weird, like that Dark Dart hoax a few years ago, when a woman was found tied onto a bed at the side of the highway claiming she'd been abducted. Police couldn't find any trace of a suspect and it slowly came out that it was a tacky publicity stunt designed to boost the career of a singer who descended into obscurity.

Anyway that's what came into my mind when I first heard the story of a 'contemporary art gallery director' in Australia with her husband 'philosopher and peer of the realm.'

Then I was at the shops getting a coke and coconut finger buns (for carbohydrate intake) and saw the front pages of the evening papers. Big black headlines:

MISSING! BRITISH ART DEALER DISAPPEARS

They're only making such a story of it as it's some aristocrat. It wasn't like that when my sister disappeared. Aphrodite joined a support group for the families of Missing Persons but nothing much came of that. Although I think it was good for her, then grandmother and grandfather died. Dad in the crash. That was it. She's been losing her memory since then.

As I walked into the newsagent I decided to buy a scraper card, it's my lucky day I thought. A pile of *Daily Demands* stacked on the counter. I handed over money and took the scraper card, and as I did looked down at front-page photos and recognized my sister with the Prime Minister.

But they had her name wrong.

It was staggering seeing her like that. Standing between the Prime Minister and a large chap, holding a champagne glass, laughing. Almost everything in her appearance was in contrast to the sister I remembered. She looked like a society type in a silky dress, made up like a television presenter. Hair stylishly dark and wavy when it used to be messy, but I knew it was her.

It was the way that she was laughing that convinced me.

Her head dipped forward slightly, with a small chunk out of her left earlobe that occurred after a home piercing.

But what was the name? Countess Ruby Rivers?
That could not be right.

'I'll buy the paper too,' I said to Peter behind the counter.

Clutching it tightly in my hand I ran home to Aphrodite, as fast as I could.

Hugo

Streets of Newcastle

'33 Rose Street, Adamstown, if you please'. No sooner had I fastened the seat belt than the interrogation began.

'You from England?'

'Yes,' I said scratching absently, gazing out at a quiet street. There was space between houses, dazzling sunlight, trees.

'Holiday?' The driver was a fellow who seemed intent on establishing a rapport.

'I suppose so,' what a holiday it was turning out to be.

'So, you like Astraea do you?'

'Hmm. Oh yes. Wonderful place.'

'So—big question, should Astraea be a Republic?'

Did I look as if I wanted to play 'Twenty Questions' with a cabdriver. 'Harrumph,' I looked out of the window, ignoring the question.

I took a swig and irritatingly as we swerved and screeched from the side of the road my head hit the window. Soon we were driving up a hill and pulling up with a jolt outside a pink cottage surrounded by palm trees .

I paid the driver, gave him a tip. But the note flew back out the window as the taxi screeched away. I bent with difficulty to retrieve the fluttering pink polymer scrap with my good hand. Walked towards the cottage, which like others I'd passed, was set by the public pavement, behind a veranda.

Given what Ruby let out about her father, little though that was, I was surprised this was her family home. If indeed it was.

Aphrodite

Nothing could have prepared me for that day.

I heard a loud knock-knock-knocking on the front door, walked down the hall, opened it and saw a large, well-dressed man with one arm in a sling, standing before me, taking up the doorway, in his white three-piece suit, sweating profusely beneath a white hat. Mopping his brow with a red and white silk spotted handkerchief and extending his hand.

'Mrs Love I presume? Good afternoon. Hugo Rivers.' His voice boomed through the heat, loud and long as foghorns of container ships on the harbour at night.

'No, I'm not Mrs Love. And I'm not Hugo Rivers either.' I stared. 'Who are you?'

Alex appeared and took over and explained to Hugo that no, I was Aphrodite Robinson, he was Alex, Rosa's brother; and, to me, that this was Hugo Rivers, Rosa's husband, he'd told me about him, and to Sir Hugo Rivers to come in. What would I do without my son? Since Rosamond disappeared. I don't know how many times did she disappear? I forget things.

Of course I always hope Rosamond will come back. That's a hope that remains as time passes.

When a child goes missing you never lose hope, but what I certainly didn't ever expect was that a strange man claiming to be her husband would appear in her place.

Especially a husband like Hugo, English, larger than life.

Alex led the way down the hall followed by the strange Englishman (I couldn't picture them together) whose huffing and puffing was quite audible.

'I don't get it,' Alex said over his shoulder. 'Where did you say you met Rosa?'

'Ruby was a student in my class at Prince's,' Hugo boomed.

'Rosa studying philosophy?' Alex sounded surprised.

'Please sit here next to the fan Hugo,' I said. He was closer in age to me than Rosamond.

'She did, she studied it exceedingly well. A most dilimphh!'

He cleared his throat noisily. Alcoholic fumes rent the air. Extraordinary. He must be mistaken; the missing Rosamond he was married to could not be our Rosa.

'In London?' asked Alex.

'Yes, London. Prince's, London.' Her supposed husband said as he sat on a pink 'Sun King' chair.

The fat alcoholic only just fitted into it.

'But how can we be sure that my daughter is your wife?' I interjected. This character wasn't going to con me in my own salon.

'Mum,' Alex sounded excited.

'You've seen the media photos. It's definitely Rosamond, I'm going to show Hugo our photos...' The visitor was staring around the living room as if in some kind of a daze.

I watched him in a gilt-framed mirror above the fireplace. A scaled-down reproduction of a mirror in Louis XVI's bedroom in the Palace of Versailles.

From my position on the loveseat, next to the Christmas tree, I had an excellent view of his reflection.

'Here, we are. The family photo albums.' Alex had brought a stack of albums from the bookshelves.

'Look Hugo—here's Roz down at the Farm, that's her first horse, Phoenix, isn't it, Mum? She would have been sixteen here, and here she is swimming, with Margarita, in the dam. We'd just had that irrigation dam dug out, above the house to water the orchard. We were filling it by pumping water from the river, it turned into a mud-bath the sides were so steep.'

'Yes,' said Hugo quietly. 'Yes that is my wife. Who is Margarita? Is she Ruby's sister?'

'No, she was Rosa's friend. She became part of our family.'

I poured the tea from the pot into three cups.

'Milk?' I asked Hugo.

'Just a little thank you.'

'Sugar?'

'Yes please.'

I passed him the heritage sugar-bowl and he helped himself. Three spoons, ladling the crystals into his tea and stirring vigorously.

'Mince pie?' I passed the plate and he took one.

'We've found her, Mum, that's why Hugo's here. He's Roz's husband! She's alive and well after all!'

'Well let's hope so.' Hugo put down his mince pie. 'Let's hope she is well. That's why I'm here after all. To meet you of course, and try to find some clues that might help us find her.'

'Dear girl,' I repeated his words. 'Do you love Rosa, Hugo?' I looked him straight in the eyes. They were heavily lidded eyes; it was impossible to tell what colour behind his glasses.

'I'm devoted to her, Aphrodite.'

'Hmmm. Well you do look different to the young artists she was involved with,' I said.

'Harrumph.' Hugo cleared his throat.

'Does Margarita live in Newcastle?'

161

'No, she's still in Sydney. She was living with Raymond for a long time. I think she's living on her own now.'

'Raymond?'

'Her boyfriend. Rosamond's boyfriend long time ago. One of her lost causes, but he settled down a lot with Margarita. Now there's a woman with a head on her shoulders.'

'Do you have Margarita's address? I'll go and visit her. She might have something, some information, a clue maybe to help give us an idea of where Ruby might be.'

'Could you fetch my handbags, please, Alex?' It can take a while finding addresses when you have handbags each with address books dating back over many years. Alex brought me my red Vesey, gold Charnel, and black Gutty. As I searched for the address book, Hugo and Alex continued talking.

'Did you say Ruby went to Art School?' Sir Hugo asked.

'Roz did, yes. For a year then she left. We've still got a stack of her paintings in the red room.'

'Her bedroom.' Sir Hugo said quietly.

'No. We named it that because of the curtains and the carpet. Roz didn't live with us. Mum and I moved up here from Sydney after Dad died. Mum didn't want to stay in the house in Glebe. When I started going to college Aphrodite moved up here too.'

'Margarita. That's where we all met Margarita. At Sterner School in Phoenix Street. Rosa, Lily, Alex, started going there when we moved from Beijing to Sydney. Her Grandfather was a violinist in Berlin Philharmonic; sent to camps in the war. A refugee in Australia. Worked as a cleaner.

They were so close people used to think they were sisters. Or lesbians,' I laughed.

'Aphrodite!' Alex said. 'She doesn't mean it,' he added.

162

'Oh Alex, loosen up, sense of humour?' I chided, turning to Hugo.

'He sent Margarita through school. Gus Minski.' I fumbled with my cuff, the hanky seemed to be stuck.

'Would you like to look at Rosa's paintings, Hugo?' Alex said brightly. What was he so upset about?

'Mum it's because of Roz that Hugo's here. We're trying to find Roz.'

'Well that's nothing new. We've been trying to find Rosa for years,' I muttered, upset by disregard for the past. The stories of our lives... Our life as the family, and Margarita's life and family. After all, she was practically my 'third daughter.' Making up for Rosamond when she vanished.

I always felt Margarita was the daughter I was supposed to have. She had practical intelligence. Rosamond was my ex-husband's daughter. Of course she was mine too, but she took after Maurice. She had that larrikin streak of his I loved and came to regret deeply.

'I would like to see Ruby's pictures, very much,' boomed the usurper, arising from the chair with some difficulty. Such a voice. I didn't like any of Roz's boyfriends. And I couldn't bring myself to like him. Why did he keep calling her Ruby?

When the man left he took all Rosamond's old paintings. Alex said he could. I wasn't sure, but Alex said it was fine; it was all 'in the family.'

Journey Back in Time

Ruby

Manguri Station, Wednesday 19 December, 2001

Manguri Station to Sydney takes three days travelling on Spirit of Progress trains. You'll need to book three tickets as you've got three legs—

Three legs, what is the woman talking about?

'There's Manguri to Adelaide, on the Bedouin; overnight trains have private sleeping compartments...'

The ticket seller delivered her spiel framed by silver tinsel draped around the ticket window. A blowfly buzzed. I had a feeling this was not quite real exacerbated by the intense heat that felt as if plates of hot steel were pressing against my head squashing my forehead, and skull.

I had caught the coach from Coober Pedy fifty kilometres into the Simpson Desert to catch the train from this outpost; no railway line in Coober. The desert stretched all directions in shimmering tangerine and violet hues. There was little else at Manguri Station beyond the train line and a station. Trains passed infrequently. I caught the coach in Coober Pedy; after walking then running from the campsite. I left Ray sleeping in the hut; I wanted to see Margy on my own, after so long. I hadn't told him I was leaving. Given that he had done something so unethical as to slip the psychedelic into my water, I did not feel any moral obligation to let him know. I wanted to leave before he might decide to do something more without asking. Besides, it was too hard to wake him.

The Bedouin Express was due in under an hour. I waited in the waiting room. The desert was beautiful but I had seen a dark side. It had brought back truths. When the train arrived I could not step up into its air-conditioned promise of escape quick enough.

Ray had given me Margy's address. I planned to surprise her. I'd seen news stands as I hurried down Coober Pedy main street in the inhuman heat. The headlines.

COUNTESS RUBY ART DISAPPEARS!

Photos of me with the Prime Minister and Hugo.

If I contacted her, Margarita might tell. I wanted to take time to find answers to questions about my missing past before I returned to Hugo and faced up to it.

As things were I didn't think that, appearance-wise, I was in danger of being recognized as Countess Ruby in the press. The photos I'd seen splashed all over the news stands were of me at DYG. I am standing with the Prime Minister, laughing, glass in hand. Over the P.M.'s shoulder, Ray is visible, in the vanishing point, at the top of a small flight of stairs. In the photo my hair is glamorously styled. In the vintage frock, Hugo's gift, I looked like a sophisticated art gallery director, a world away from where I was in a lonely train carriage rolling through the desert.

Clad in Ray's jeans and tee shirt emblazoned with a dead rose (none-too-clean). I'd borrowed his big bushman hat and wore it low to hide sight of my face under the wide brim. My hair sticky-thick with red dust I pulled forward over my face, ochre curtains, when anyone came near I lowered my head.

When I saw the reflection in the mirror above the wash-hand basin in the toilet cubicle, I gasped. What a fright.

I didn't have any make-up. As I always wore a thick mask of cosmetics, my natural face was hard enough to recognize at the best of times. But the face that stared back at me was of a wild woman. Skin burnt red by the desert sun, nose peeling. Lips blistered.

Eyes staring as if under influence of drugs, which I was not, at least I hoped not. I needed fluids to flush out all traces of the poison.

All I wanted was to be myself, to be strong, think clearly. I swore to myself I would never take another drug again. My mind was sandblasted, finding my way around a raw mental landscape bumping into things, confused.

Hugo? Now and then thoughts of my husband stole into my mind but it seemed impossible to reconcile him anywhere in this picture at the present.

All I could think about was Margarita. Did she still smell the same? The natural musky perfume of her skin that I had secretly loved, she had her own exotic fragrance.

As I remember Margarita, the sound of her violin swirls into my mind; I hear her playing that old sweet music. The fugue she used to play. I close my eyes and my thoughts begin to drift.

I'm awoken from reverie by chewing in my ear. As I dozed a large smiling person moved into the seat beside me. A magazine is open on her knees but she is not reading. She is using it as a plate. She smiles at me, mouth full, as she pulls a breadstick from her bag.

Sighing, I turn to look at the desert.

High in the sky clouds so surreal they make Dali look like photo-realism.

After a while I turn, see her smiling at me, I wanly smile back. Then I notice the image on the page on her lap. It's me! With Hugo and the Australian Prime Minister. Any minute she might look down, focus, notice. Despite my reluctance to move about, I have to find a new seat.

'Excuse me,' I embarrassingly almost fall into her bosom as I squeeze past.

In the next carriage, I find a window seat. Put my bag and backpack into the spare seat beside it and fall asleep. At some indeterminate point my eyes open.

There are camels ambling through the desert next to the train.

I wake properly. The flatness of the desert is beginning to give way to ripples, red dust of the ground tinged very faintly with green. The train-line veers close to the road.

Against the skyline is half a house, on the back of a truck, being driven through the desert.

On its way to where? I wonder. Looking for its other half? I drift back into sleep.

The train arrives in Adelaide hours before the connection.

Walking the platform, memories of the time I was here push into mind. The three of us drove to the station. Ray and I picked up Margarita at the Castle, that house full of broken dreams, men who drifted up and down the stairs, like ghosts. For once none of us had anything to say. Nothing we were able to say, anyway. The day felt heavy, dull with finality, anti-climax. There seemed to be very little time. Ray carrying my suitcases. Margy looking worried, hurrying beside. Ray helping me onto the train with my luggage. No one making light of it, unable to make a quip, a joke. Not knowing what's happened exactly only that I must go. As far away as possible. As I walk through the station, my mind fills with images.

The last image from the window of the train carrying me away. Ray in black jeans, jumper; shock of red hair; Margarita in a dark 1940s dress. I watched the fingers of his hand fluttering like petals of a flower blowing in the wind.

In a moment they were gone.

The two people I loved intensely.

I was gone.

I walk past news stands where my image is displayed and keep my head turned to the ground.

The train is about to leave. I booked a sleeping compartment. Although I slept for hours on the first train, all I want to do is lie down, close my eyes and fall into oblivion.

I find my compartment, and go to sleep.

Later I wake to see Hay Plains. A golden rippling sea of wheat shining in the evening light beyond the window.

My throat is parched, veins dried out. My skin feels dry and itchy as if burnt inside, I need water. Feels like my body's filled with red dust, toxins that if I'm lucky I will flush out. I stand up, walk to the buffet, join a queue of people waiting to be served at a counter which is festooned with red and silver tinsel.

As I wait, leaning against the wall, a man comes up.

'This is the buffet I take it,' his voice is soft, evenly pitched.

'Yes,' I turn towards him. He is probably about forty, and has piercing blue eyes. He's looking at me curiously; of course he couldn't recognize me. I look horrendous, and do not feel better. Must drink. Drink. Drink.

'Two orange juices, three bottles of water, and a coffee.'

I hurry with my head down through the carriages. Drink and drink until water and juice is gone. Rehydrated, I take off my bra from under Ray's tee shirt pulling it out of one of the armholes; as if I'm changing on a beach. Then I take off Ray's jeans. Sip the coffee.

I unfold a bed down from the wall collapse on a cushioned surface, turn out the light and give in to sleep.

At some point I wake up and hurry to the bathroom, need to flush out the toxins, all that fluid. I drink some more.

At Melbourne station I disembark. 7.45 a.m.. There's only fifteen minutes before the next train to Sydney leaves.

As I weave through mechanical crowds of commuters I find myself. Right before me, is me, at DYG with the Prime Minister and Hugo, I am laughing. I look around, there I am again, on another news stand. I am everywhere smiling on the front pages of newspapers, as if in a hall of mirrors.

I look up. He's standing still in the crowd staring at me. The man who was at the buffet counter on the train.

'Excuse me,' he says hurrying towards me, a guitar case in his hand. All I can think of is flight. Run, Ruby run.

I grab the straps of the backpack and take off through the madding crowd. I run weaving my way onto a busy pavement of a city street pass an open bar and rush in through the door. The bartender glances at me. I hold my head high but turned away, hoping he will assume I am a hotel guest about to buy breakfast. I walk a straight line to the ladies, and hide in there long enough for my heart to stop pounding.

By the time I feel it's safe enough to head back out onto the street to the station I've missed the train.

The next train left at 7.30 p.m.. Ten hours in Melbourne.

What to do? I can't stay in the station of strange yet familiar men with blue eye. And news stands.

Someone would identify me.

Someone might recognise me.

Margarita

16, The Mayfair, Wednesday 19 December, 2001

I had my hair cut. I'd been thinking about it for months, then walking home from work instead of going the usual way I left the main road and walked down the Glebe Point Road. There was a salon I knew of staffed by women with attitude and no hair. I'd go there and get it done, now.

The stylist standing behind me smoothed my hair with her hands. She had no hair, and wore that season's inner-city dyke's uniform: black tee shirt, indigo jeans. A chain dangled jangling from the ring in her nostril to a ring in her ear. Later when she dried my hair she banged my head with the blow dryer like it was cool. (I didn't think so).

She picked up scissors and made the first cut at the back of my neck, a thirty-centimetre tress of black hair fell to the ground. Snip-snip-snip, at the nape of my neck. She gestured to an assistant who swept it up and put it into a plastic bag. No doubt they use high quality long hair for wigs, I thought. My hair could end up shaking down the street in Mardi Gras.

I emerged, blinking. Gone were the curly locks, now I had a sharp crew cut. I glanced at my reflection in windows as I strode along George Street. Despite my plumpness, I felt pleased by my new appearance. A breeze caressed my neck. My head was light. It felt as if a heavy weight had fallen from me which it had. My hair had gone, my hair which held the past like a shroud. My hair, which had held his kisses, and rough hands. I felt light and free as if I'd escaped from a dangerous fate, as if with a few clean cuts I could leave Raymond behind.

Two days later, the feeling of light optimism, excitement remains.

Now when I return home, and undress in the apartment, look at myself in the mirror, it's as if I am looking at a new person. Marguerite. My old vulnerable female self has gone. That self that was abused and criticized by Ray. If he were to see me now, I am convinced he would not even be attracted to me, he might be intimidated by me now I've finally got the hair-cut to match my suit. Now I look so much like a dyke.

I run my hand over my scalp, through short stiff bristles, the spiky ends of my hair, over and over again.

Ruby

Streets of Melbourne

I walked from the station and turned left, as if following an automatic imperative, letting my feet find the way. Of course this was the way I walked when I was going to stay with Margy, when she lived in the stable. Studying photography. I was studying in Adelaide. I would always walk to her place from the station for exercise, to stretch my legs after the muscle-cramping overnight train (no sleeping compartments for me then); I was following the route without thinking. My feet remembered. It was a hot morning. I was covered in sweat.

As I walked, breathing heavily, little by little a cinematic track of underground forgotten events swirled into my mind. Memories emerging like a transfer revealing its colours, like images of deceased lords and ladies in a brass rubbing in an old church, just the right amount of pressure yields the perfect image. The pressure applied by my walking legs, my feet on the ground of streets after the long train journey, a ride on a ghost train. I was breathing the air of these same long-forgotten streets, reinvesting the sights, smells, atmosphere with new life.

I remembered his departure from the station here. He had caught the train back to Adelaide. I had said good-bye to him at this same station, Flinders Street, with longing and regret.

Why couldn't I just go with him? Why couldn't I tell him I'd go with him to his cousin's in the rainforest? Why couldn't I tell him what I really thought, and act on it?

Why had I been so torn?

As I reached the turning to the street Margarita had lived on, I walked past the traffic island on the quiet street where Ray and I had a picnic together one hot summer's night, and lay on our backs gazing into the sky, finding constellations of the big dipper and little dipper, memories ricochet into mind with the force of absolute certainty.

By the time I reach the entrance to the stable-yard where she lived I am dripping with sweat. My back aching from the weight of the backpack, my shoulder is frozen. But none of that means anything to me now.

I gaze at the gates in front of the stable-apartments where she had lived. How I had liked to visit her.

That time we spent here with Ray, all three of us sleeping in her large bed. I had seen it as friendship; we were close enough to sleep together. If one is your best friend and the other your partner I thought, all the more reason for it to be all right, for sleeping to be chaste.

Then I discovered that, all that time, Margarita had been soliciting his attention, making up lies, things she said to him about 'all' my boyfriends that made him assume I had been driven to his cousin's place by my so-called 'latest boyfriend' when instead I had risked my life to hitch-hike to visit him.

Do Re Mi

I had been attracted to Ray from the first moment I saw him, at a party for fresher art students, held at the student house I had moved into opposite a funfair, back from the beach in Glenelg. Neville held the lease. He was the Art School social secretary and had thrown the party. As soon as I saw the red haired man dressed in black, dancing and laughing, I could not take my eyes off him. It was as if he was surrounded by a magnetic force field of energy that repelled some and attracted others.

'That's Raymond Furness' said Neville, at my elbow.

'One of the leather jacket boys. They call themselves Art Criminals, a bunch of fourth years. They go around creating a public disturbance, and they call it art.'

A few days later Raymond moved into the house where I was living with my de facto Wolfie who was supposed to have just dropped me off and then gone back to Sydney as we had split up after living together for years since I was seventeen and kicked out of home as my parents didn't like him. But Wolfie was still around, and now Raymond was living in the house, he had moved in with Lily (not my sister, another Lily) who also met him at the party. I couldn't keep my eyes off him, I saw him in the kitchen or living room. I heard him with Lily as they were in the next room to mine. Everything he left lying around, books, *Gold of the Tigers,* art comics, I found myself picking up, looking at as if they were sacred fetish objects of a tribe that I was interested in, the conceptual art tribe though I did not know it then. Then Ray and Lily split up. They each moved out, but I still saw him around at the endless parties and happenings.

An end of the year party was held at the big house a couple of doors down. I went with Wolfie who was still sharing my room. Ray and the Art Criminals were there. Wolfie only went back to our house after he thought Ray had left.

But I knew Ray had only gone to buy drugs as he had told me, and I stayed willing to see him later. I was not interested in the drugs. I didn't do drugs. I had exchanged magnetically charged words with him before he left.

When Ray returned hidden mutual attraction brought us together in a most intense way. I'd been hoping, willing, this would happen all year. We danced, kissed, and made love in a cupboard on a landing that held a water heater, and so our passionate romance began.

I told Wolfie and he left, after five days, a time in which our wills battled silently. He packed up the panniers and departed on his motorbike. Now, I thought, I was free to love as deeply, and as passionately, meaningfully, as things would go with Raymond. However I had not counted on the arrival of Margarita. Wolfie stayed with her in Melbourne after he left. He failed to mention to her that I was with someone else.

Margarita stayed five long days and nights with Ray and me, right at the start of my relationship with him, the most precious formative time. I felt I could not ask her to leave as she was my best friend, but all I wanted to do was tell her to

174

leave, let me get on with my new relationship. She was in my relationship; there were always three of us, although I did not see it then.

As things ended I had to acknowledge. Although I vowed never to return whilst they were together. Ironically, they had recently separated following ten years together.

My telepathic power, or intuition, that helped me discover artists as an art writer, and dealer, was still working.

What good it would do me now though I did not know.

I wondered when I'd see Raymond again.

The afternoon Wolfie left Raymond came to the house, as neither of us had a phone we had not been in contact.

'Wolfie's gone,' I gazed into his pale blue eyes. Our lips met and it was as electric as the first time. I fell into his kisses and it was like hurtling down the slide on the big dipper, I didn't want this to stop, I wanted to fall, screaming, waving my arms in the air like this forever. We went into my room. Made love on the mattress on the floor.

In the evening we wandered over to the bottle-shop. Ray bought a bottle of South Australian Shiraz. We walked down to the beach and lay on warm sand, drank the purple wine. I laughed because the wine had stained Ray's lips black; and he said it had done the same, to my lips. The sun slipped into the sea, setting the purple water alight.

'This is so romantic,' he said.

'It's like being in the tunnel of love,' I laughed.

'Instead of watching a film we're watching the real thing.'

'Stretched out in front of us an unrepeatable gift of nature.'

'You, me and the wine-dark sea,' Ray put his arm around my waist and pulled me closer to him.

'I want to drown with you, baby,' I hoped it sounded ironic not cheesy.

The light faded, a big yellow summer milk moon rose up from the rim of the glittering ocean. When it was dark, the breeze off the Bay freshened, we returned to the house. I forgot about dinner. Ray didn't mention it. We made love again on my bed, and fell asleep in each other's arms.

'Don't die' said Raymond, one evening a few days later.

'What?'

'Now I've found you, I don't want to lose you. You'd better not die on me.'

'I won't,' I laughed lightly.

But I didn't say how much his words disturbed me. Did he mean 'die' figuratively, symbolically, or —surely not—literally? Where was his doubt coming from? Did I look unwell? I had a deep fear of death.

Ray drove me in his parent's car to the University on the edge of the city for me to drop off my last assignments and then it was over. I had completed First Year.

'Freedom!' I said, laughing, as we zoomed away in the car. In my feverish projection, the prospect of enchanted summer was rolling exorbitantly, shimmering, a gift of azure light and heat, it felt sensual, sensational, the embodied desire of a lover's mirage. A gift I could hardly believe was mine.

Rimbaud watched from the window as Verlaine ran out onto the street, blood was dripping from his hand...Beside him a belly dancer...Twenty camels and Lawrence of Arabia who, before anyone noticed or could stop it from happening, had gone native in his turban and Bedouin robes reclining on hot sand beside his camel...

We ventured out of my room half-dressed into the kitchen at Rubicon Road. Screeching cicadas, hot night. We had been in the house alone, our palace of delights and violently tender pleasures, not gone out for three days and nights.

Everyone else had vanished. In the end the house of artists, which had begun with friendly promise, had disintegrated.

Raymond and I were sole survivors of a shipwreck washed up on a desert island... The lease was about to end, we must leave soon. I hadn't yet made a decision on where to spend summer. Sydney, the Farm, Margarita's in Melbourne. I was here 'in the moment', with Ray, the here and the now, that's all I was thinking of.

Living in my senses, my body. The universe condensed into a sigh, shared inner world of feeling, where intense meaning was inscribed in thoughts by signs, such as the flicker of his eye, tenor of voice. As if writing a body poem, I mapped his every freckle with the tips of my fingers and tongue, I traced a constellation of marks, the language of his life tattoos. I was trying to solder his image in memory. I was discovering the physical coastline of a whole new artist's continent.

The shape of Ray's bones, his wiriness, entranced me; he was not much taller than I.

I had lost my appetite for food and he didn't seem to want to eat either. For days, we lived on each other's bodies.

As we stood in the kitchen, nibbling toast like penitents, Ray said, 'I think I'll set out for Grafton in the next week or so, hitch a ride in a truck, or catch a train. My cousin's place is about forty kilometres from Grafton in mid-northern New South Wales, rainforest. He and Nita, his girlfriend, are living in a barn. They built the barn; the shack where I'll be painting my works of genius is downhill from their place. It should be a blast, baby... You still want to come with me?' His voice was hesitant.

A week? Ray had mentioned some plans but I couldn't get my mind around it. 'Uh, yeah, okay, I think so,' I said.

I couldn't visualize Rex, or Grafton.

The prospect of summer rippled through my thoughts, a vast expanse of beach beneath the blinding blue-sky brilliant vista of the Bay, filled with light. My projections had about as much substance as fairy floss but like a kid at the fairground I didn't want the ride to end.

Plans, particularly those involving other people, would end what we had here, and propel us back into a normal life that I didn't want to re-enter yet. I wanted us to stay enclosed in a private bubble of love. I did not want anything or anyone else but him.

'I've told Rex I might be travelling with a Beautiful Lady.' His tone was coaxing, hands lightly caressed my waist. He was looking at me intently.

'That's you.' I loved his humour, sophistication. But I had an uncertain feeling.

Although I didn't manage a verbal reply, I made an effort to smile. We started to kiss. I knew that whatever happened would be all right. One night, early in that year on the beach my lucky star had promised everything would work out fine.

We awoke mid-morning. I arose, went to the bathroom, drank a glass of water, went back to bed. We made love on the mattress in burning beams of sunlight.

'You look like an angel,' he said.

My eyes were semi-closed against sun rays slanting at angles across the room.

Everything shimmered in the intense light. Kneeling on his heels above me, haloed by blinding light pouring through the window. His bronze hair set alight by the sun.

'We recognized each other,' he said.

Miraculously, I thought.

And then the doorbell started to ring.

'Just ignore it.' It kept ringing, and ringing.

'Someone is persistent.'

I stood up, swaying on the mattress, wrapping the sheet round me, toga-style.

'I'll just go and see who that is.'

Swathed in the sheet, I walked out of the bedroom, down the hallway and opened the front door.

Medusa

5 Rubicon Rd, Glenelg, Adelaide, years before

Surprise!! Margarita was standing on the doorstep. Dressed in a black tunic with white collar, black ankle-boots. Black hat under which twitched dreadlocks.

'Wolfie said you've split up! He stayed at my place on his way to Sydney. He was upset! Said you were having a break. So you did it—well done, Rosa-baby!'

I couldn't believe it. I gazed in horror—those dreadlocks! What was my best friend doing here? She pushed past me into the hall. I grabbed her arm.

'Did Wolfie tell you I'm with Raymond now?' I hissed in her ear.

'What? No!!' Her voice went flat. She stared, unguarded and deflated. I wanted to say: please go, but I couldn't do that.

'I'll just go and tell Raymond you're here. He's been staying with me for a week, since Wolfie left.'

I stared at her, willing her to read my thoughts, to guess I am in love, it is bad timing and I just want to be alone with my love. I willed her to say she would leave us, get on the next twelve-hour train back to Melbourne, and good luck with my new relationship. But she didn't.

She took two steps into the hallway. Brandishing her case.

'Uh, okay, hold on, I'll just go and get dressed,' I said.

I shuffled back into my bedroom and closed the door.

Ray was sitting on the bed, looking puzzled.

'Margarita's here,' I whispered, dropping the sheet.

'What?' He looked more puzzled.

'Margarita? Where did she come from?"

'She's come to visit. Wolfie told her we split up. He stayed with her at her place in Melbourne on his way back to Sydney. He didn't tell her about you. She's got dreadlocks.' I said sotto voce.

Ray looked bemused. He stood and began to pull on his black trousers.

I slipped into my black skirt and purple vest from the pile of clothes flung over my worktable. After turning to smile at him again, I entered another mode, walked out of the room. I had to look after my friend. Make tea; fix a bed for her on the couch in the hall where she slept when she came here to stay; think about lunch. All the normal things that I'd wanted to forget about for a bit longer.

'When did you decide to get dreadlocks?' I asked as we sat around sipping tea.

'Oh!' Margy laughed. She reached up to her head, grabbed a few locks and started tugging and yanking at her own hair. I watched her in surprise, Ray watched her warily.

Suddenly she pulled even harder and scalped herself.

I stared at her blankly.

'It's a wig!' Margy screamed.

'From the second-hand theatrical shop!'

Under the wig her real hair was fastened with hair-grips.

'Oh God, the looks of yer faces, I'm pissin' me sel'—

She exaggerated her Irish accent as she often did to amuse us, cracking up with laughter and clutching her midriff, she ran out from the kitchen, into the bathroom next door.

'Hmm!' Ray smiling picked up the wig; put it on his head, and started cackling with laughter; Margarita came back into the kitchen unpinning her natural locks.

'Shure, it's very fetching on you Furness. Ye should wear yer hair in skinny wee bunches, like that, all the time, mon!' Her long glossy black hair tumbled down over her face.

For the next days the three of us spent our time together. Margarita came everywhere with Raymond and me. Walks, to shops. To an opening at the Photographers' Gallery. To a party held by one of Ray's former lecturers. Ray and I stopped walking to the beach in the evenings with a bottle of wine. Every conversation we had in the open, she was there—joining in. She wanted to talk with him about art, photography, music, people, film, books, ideas…anything. I started to think that he was her main attraction. My feelings of intense desire for my new lover (annoyingly) made me slightly tongue-tied with him even in intimacy.

And now Margarita was monopolizing every one of our conversations, in a way she would not have been able to do if Ray was Wolfie. I thought that I could understand her behaviour because of that. She was making up for lost time.

After all the four and a half years I lived with Wolfie and she was hardly able to speak to me in his company as he did not like me to spend too much of my time with her let alone have long conversations.

With Margarita buzzing around I was finding it harder to think about summer plans. The idea of going to Grafton with Ray was becoming ever more difficult to envisage. If I went to Grafton with Ray, what would Margarita do?

She was suddenly apparently relying on me to provide her with suitable summer arrangements.

I'd had enough of thinking and talking; I brought out palette and canvases and began to paint.

I painted three people, the three of us, on the porch of the house opposite a funfair, after Margy arrived. Ray had made a cocktail he'd invented: vodka and blackberry nip. I painted his image as if reflected in the Hall of Mirrors in the fairground over the road. His image flattened and foreshortened. Dressed in black. His red hair, nimbus of barbed wire spikes, dead-white pallor of his face. Swinging the vodka bottle.

I painted her bellowing with laughter, spitting a mouthful of vodka and blackberry nip in an arc of light-filled droplets—

She knew I was upset, as I jumped up and rushed into the house, but she didn't know quite how mad I was at her little joke, which he seemed to find so funny.

It was one of our last evenings, the first of early summer, the air fresh, clear. The violet sky and clouds flaming apricot, pink, gold in a paradox of sunset, which as its beauty becomes more intensely fleeting looks as if it must go on forever.

Or is it because it is ephemeral and eternal, that the drama of sun's daily disappearance appears beautiful. We perceive it as uplifting rather than as a terrible display of the power of nature. Or was that the illusion of my youth.

An evening that should be perfect but it wasn't because my friend was there and I couldn't forget her by losing myself as I wanted to. Drinking with Ray in the evening luminescence, alone. Two lovers flying into space-lands together. Already I was addicted to an intoxicating cocktail of Ray-and-booze.

I could not attempt to disappear into states of bliss with Ray. What would be the point with Margarita hovering, just waiting for the chance to spit vodka and blackberry nip?

And now it was all over. The lease was up we had to leave.

I packed up, cleaned out my room. Ray had been living in his parents' garage (though he had been staying at my house for the past days). I could not stay with him there as he said they would not allow that. I decided to go with Margarita to Melbourne and then to my family house, in Glebe, in Sydney. When I was sorting out my things I picked up a typewritten sheet from my desk.

A stanza from a poem by Anna Akhmatova.

I read the words slowly, how beautiful. One day I'd like to try to do something with that idea in an artwork.

I slipped the lines between pages of my notebook, and put it into my army bag with notes I was saving for I didn't know what kind of posterity.

The day before we left the house a letter arrived, addressed to me in Wolfie's handwriting. I opened it to find a letter he'd written at Margy's. He'd arrived unannounced and she was not there.

At the end of his letter were a few lines penned in a larger, looser and equally familiar hand:

> Well hi baby—the lost wanderer has at last returned from a weekend in Prahran and a day at the seaside only to find the Wolfe in me bed! What a surprise-shure is grand to be seein' the lad again. I hear yuz have been havin a wee separation for a while— a good idea I think but I bet your marbles it won't last long. My god today is so fucking hot. ...I am meaning always to visit in a couple of days or weeks but always something comes up, a job, music practice or an exam —always something to keep me here. But my plan, which I shall have to hurry cos Big Wolfie is itching

to go and post this, is to come down next week-end and stay a week or so by the sea so what I shall do is wait until you send me your very prompt reply to say when you will depart Adelaide. I might even be able to come on Wed. but then I'll wait till I hear from you cos Wolfie says it was in your wee head to leave on Friday for good and all [the first I had heard of it...]

So dwarling, write to tell me what you want to do— it would be nice to stay a week after exams should it not? Anyway write soon & tell me what you're doing. I'm not sure what I'm doing about moving, I'd like to move to the seaside, but the idea of shifting all my stuff does not exactly appeal.

I shall save all the gossip for when I see you in the near future.

So write <u>immediately</u>, priority paid mail & say the word—<u>OK</u>.

Hope you are in good shape.

All my love

Margy xxxxxxx

Sorry for not having written.

Reading the words produced a sensation of being caught in a time-space warp.

Instead of being seven hundred and twenty five kilometres apart as propriety dictated that we should be, Margarita was tucking into her breakfast fruit and yogurt but a few metres away. Well, it was too late to say to her not to visit now.

'Guess what's just arrived?' I waved her missive as I paced the living room.

'Oh, have you only just got it?' she said, looking shocked,

then starting to laugh.

She must have left Melbourne as soon as she posted it. Far from waiting for my reply, she had decided to surprise me, and just turn up, take the overnight train and arrive. Not thinking that I could be with a new lover.

'It's just arrived,' I said.

I felt like an unsuspecting recipient of a date-rape drug in the urban myth who supposedly opens her eyes, to find she is tied up, and asks her assailant, 'what are you going to do?'

And the woman says to her, it's already happened.

But, Margy may have felt the same way.

I was determined to show I was no one's victim.

Melbourne Heat

It was not cold in Melbourne. I'd been there a week with Margy staying at her place in Carlton. Sleeping next to her, in the overstuffed lumpy double bed. Under the tin roof, the stable where she was living heated up like a toaster.

Raymond arrived in the middle of the night. I was expecting him. He'd written to me after I left, said he wanted to visit me in Melbourne; couldn't wait to see me in Sydney. I was sleeping as was Margy but the banging woke me. I jumped out of her bed, naked. I always slept naked when it was hot.

I walked to the stable door in the kitchen and opened it, unbolting and swinging open the top door first, and then the bottom.

Ray was standing there, an expression of shock on his face.

'Hi,' I said.

He stared at me blankly without saying anything.

'Ray? Are you all right? Is there anything wrong?'

186

'You're not wearing anything!' Ray said without moving.

'So what's wrong with that!' I laughed.

'Come in.' He stepped inside and I closed the doors.

'It's Australia! Nudity is not exactly a big deal!'

I had been to Back-to-Earth Festivals where thousands of people congregated and swam naked in the river, a statement against the supposed hypocrisy of clothes-wearing in society and literal bid to strip off social conditioning, although I hadn't gone that far. I'd gone halfway: topless.

I had been to two festivals with friends. I assumed anyone who was or wanted to be an artist, freethinker and free spirit in Australia must be part of the naturist-friendly movement. A Labour Deputy Prime Minister founded the festival; many believed an enlightened new era was dawning. My Grandmother was interested to talk to me on the telephone about the back-to-earth festivals and the nudity they endorsed. My parents didn't exactly approve but didn't stop me going, they had been concerned.

But Ray was a conceptual artist. I was privately shocked that he looked shocked. Nudity amongst friends was all about transcending, inhibitions and social conditioning.

'So how are you?' I said.

'My head aches...' His voice was faint. 'I'm wrecked, mate, hitchhiked from just outside Adelaide, Tailem Bend, there were trucks at the service station. Been sitting in a truck for nine hours straight. The truckie gave me some of his pills, they did my head in.'

'Let me show you around Margarita's stable,' I said.

'The kitchen-dining-work room!' I gestured around me.

'The bedroom!'

He followed me. To save embarrassment I slipped into an

eau-de-nil 1920s silk nightdress that I grabbed from a pile of clothes.

He looked even more puzzled.

'There's nowhere else to sleep, Ray.'

I jumped into bed, in the middle. He took off his clothes and joined me. He left on his boxers, I noticed in amusement.

Margarita didn't wake up.

The heat wave arrived next day. We all woke up drenched in sweat. Above us the roof was creaking and cracking as the iron contracted in the soaring mid-morning temperature.

Ray pulled on his shorts and his Lone Deranger tee shirt. I tied my blue and white batik-patterned sarong around my hip, slipped into my purple vest.

I was surprised Margarita was wearing my mother's old slip that she teamed flamboyantly with stockings. I watched her, not sure whether to be amused, as she tottered across the cobbles to the washhouse and laundry shared by occupants of the stable-apartments. Margy had not liked Back-to-Earth festivals. Punk she picked up on straight away.

'So, how's work going?' I asked as we were eating breakfast of fruit, yogurt and percolated coffee.

'Pretty good,' he replied.

'When I go back I'll finish the Faces project and take it to the gallery. Then I'll set out my cousin's place in the rainforest to paint there. I'll meet you here or we can meet in Sydney, what do you think?'

I was thinking about going to the rainforest with Ray, and was just about to say so when Margarita butted in, as if he was talking to her.

'First I have to withdraw from my course,' she said.

She stood up and deliberately casually flipped up her slip.

188

She adjusted her tights. Ray must be able to see, I thought. But Margy appeared to be looking straight at Ray.

Her gesture was in the brazen spirit of punk we pretended we weren't embodying and, as I'd felt several times since her arrival into my relationship with Ray, I wasn't sure whether to feel amused or annoyed by her new behaviour.

'I'll do it this week, then I'll pack up my stuff and move out of here,' she said airily. I noticed that Ray had noticed.

'It's okay to leave it at your Mum's isn't it?' She looked at me.

'Yeah,' I said without much enthusiasm.

I was wishing I could go back to Adelaide with Ray, which I couldn't as he was living in his parents' garage.

He'd said they would not approve of my joining him in his garage hideaway. I knew what it looked like I had visited Ray there with Wolfie. A single mattress on a concrete floor flanked by old white-goods, furniture, and the family car. So, instead, I had to stay in limbo with Margarita in her stable.

Languid in the intimate heat I dreamily watched her apply her make-up. Squinting at her reflection in a shaving mirror on the table, head tilted back exposing the curve of her throat; she draws a line around her eye with kohl pencil. Stretching the skin of her eyelid with her fingers. With deft flicks of her '50s powder puff, she teases her cheeks and nose. Absorbing a layer of whitish sunscreen-shine. Baring her teeth she rings her mouth with magenta lipstick pushed against her full lips. She studies her handiwork for a moment then zips cosmetics in a fluffy pink case that she pops into her army surplus store bag. She applied her make up with movements that were precise, definite. In the self-construction of her bold persona, as many of our friends Margarita perfected the art of exaggerated theatricality of a fairground sideshow actor, with the precision of a circus performer. Soon I would be too.

She pouted, smacking lips noisily in exaggerated kisses.

'Okay darlings!' She trilled. 'I'm going out now. Got to see Derrida about busking. I'll be back this afternoon! Be good!' Picking up parasol and bag she clattered away, dreadlocks twitching. Mum's black slip shining, glossy, sleek. Nevermore, I thought. If Margy were a bird she'd be a raven.

As soon as clacking of her tap dancing shoes receded into the distance, Ray and I returned to bed.

The temperature reminded me of the first time. Already that seemed a long time ago.

'Do you remember that little room?' I said, as he pounded.

I wanted to believe our feelings were becoming ever more intense and crystalline, the longer I was with him.

Ray wanted to go to the National Gallery of Victoria.

We set off at midday, walking into a city of metallic light. Melbourne looked as if it was melting into a new combination of chemistry elements, silver, copper, platinum, gold laser-rays of light; houses, buildings, traffic, refracted blinding alchemical light-heat waves.

The smell of bushfires hung in the air.

'Whoa,' Ray said reeling.

The streets were deserted. The city becalmed at 48 degrees Celsius. In Adelaide when it was very hot as I stared into the glassy Bay *Like a painted ship upon a painted ocean*[15] a line from Coleridge's *Rhyme of the Ancient Mariner* came into mind. The stationary yachts marooned on glittering water evoked a solipsistic universe where deep communication is impossible. But that was before I had found Ray.

190

I wanted to think that the reality of us walking together now through this furnace turned heat into a surreal sensual experience. Towards town, we passed middle aged women on the street holding onto the bars of fences, like swimmers in trouble clutching onto life buoys.

We walked into a shop. The two young Greek guys handed us wrong change for bottles of water we bought.

We were undercharged.

Everyone was dazed by the heat. But there was an uncanny air of expectation as if now that temperature had exceeded all reasonable limits anything else could happen...

The city could be invaded, looted, pillaged by marauders.

Fireballs could spontaneously combust in the air, bowling down the street.

Visions of extreme transformative beauty, what we know we want, could materialize trembling, bathed in golden light, before our eyes.

The gallery was air-conditioned; we stayed there for hours.

We returned to Margarita's early evening, with a bottle of wine. She wasn't there. The stable was stifling, airless. It was too hot to cook and there was nothing to cook with. I made a salad with greens and cheese from the fridge, dry remains of a loaf of bread.

'Do you want to go to that park down the road,' said Ray after we'd finished eating. He was referring to the grassy area with bushes on a pedestrian traffic island in the middle of the road. It would have never occurred to me to go there. But it was a back street and very quiet.

'Let's take a blanket to lie on,' he said.

I laughed. I thought he was joking.

'No. It's a thing to do. Like sleeping outdoors in the garden when you're a kid in summer, setting up for a picnic.'

'All these cultural traditions I'm finding out about.'

I laughed.

We reclined on the blanket, drank burgundy and lay on our backs staring up at smoky smog trying to detect stars.

Next morning, Margarita was still not back.

And the temperature was, if possible, even higher.

'Let's go to St Kilda. Have a swim. Cool down.' I said.

'Yep, Sounds good,' Ray said.

We caught the tram there, but when we arrived at the sea-front, we found much of the fit population of Melbourne had been inspired by the same idea. The beach was blanketed with shiny comatose bodies, stretched out on the sand and towels, basting beneath the sun. Acres of red-brown flesh lubricated by oils and lotions sizzled and steamed tenderly. The air redolent of coconut oil. The sea full of bodies but everyone seemed to be standing still or splashing feebly, too hot to move. We sought shelter in a pavilion on the sand, it was shaded but hot. I took off my sarong, leaving on vest and black undies (I hadn't worn swimmers or a bikini since I threw out make-up and heels and went back to earth).

'I'm not going in, sport, I'm going to stay here,' said Ray, his face pink and glistening.

He sat down, and pulled out a visual diary from his back-pack. The sand was burning hot. I ran across it to prevent the soles of my feet scalding.

The water was glassy, torpid; it made me think of opaque yellow-green jelly. I dived under, hoping I'd cool down. But the water was almost as hot as the air.

'Let's find a pub,' Ray said, when I returned.

'Good idea.'

The pub was cool, air conditioned, and we stayed there a couple of hours. I sipped beer sitting close to Ray sipping beer, in front of us large tinted windows, we gazed.

Margarita was back at her place when we returned, buzzing around, laughing and talking at high speed, looking totally refreshed.

'I went to a nightclub on the roof of the Spiral, after I went busking with Derrida. Met a chap, Aspen College, good look-ing; invited me back to his parent's house. His parents were away; their *mansion* in Toorak had a pool. I've just endured two days of torture lounging around, having cocktails brought to me by gorgeous young men...'

I stared at her in disgust.

'God. And I was worried something bad had happened to you,' I said. 'We've hardly been able to move in this heat. Are you going to see him again?'

'No,' she said, tossing her dreadlocks.

I saw what I wanted to interpret as a 'split-second' look, an expression of hidden pain, as she glanced at Ray then me and walked out of her bedroom, spike heels click-clacking on the old worn linoleum.

The next day Ray planned to go back to Adelaide to finish preparing work for his exhibition. Margarita and I were going to take a train to Sydney. We were going to stay at Mum's terrace house in Glebe. Ray would call in and visit on his way up to Grafton.

I still hadn't decided about going to his cousin's place in

the rainforest. I tried to talk about it with Margarita when he was out at the shops buying milk. But she wouldn't talk to me about it.

'It's your decision,' she said so tartly it made me wonder.

She wouldn't look at me, and flounced out of her bedroom dreadlocks twitching. There was certainly something upsetting her.

As it was his last night in Melbourne, the three of us went to Ronny's Greenroom, a poolroom bar Margy had found. We ordered drinks and sat in the green-lit shadows.

Margy was refreshed. I was sunburnt and dazed. Although I was sitting with her and Ray, I felt like I was the audience watching a diva performing on stage. In irritation I looked at her black-and-purple velvet bodice, plunging neckline, cobalt lips, dreadlocks. Her voice rang; laughter that could have shattered glass.

I shifted my gaze to rectangles of smoky green light, the pool room visible. Shapes of players moving slowly, circling pool sharks.

She couldn't get enough of laughing and talking—with Ray.

Ten years later and now I knew.

By the time I reach her old stable-yard I am dripping with sweat. My back is aching from the weight of the pack and my left shoulder frozen. But none of that means anything to me.

When I thought Margy was my friend she was trying to steal my lover. No wonder everything went wrong with her and me. She was trying to put him off, turn him against me.

I gazed at black metal gates that led into the stables where she had lived. How I had liked to visit her here.

I discovered she had been soliciting his attention, making up things, what had she said to him about 'all' my boyfriends that had led to his ridiculous false assumption that I had been driven to his cousin's by my 'new boyfriend' ('Tony') when in reality I had risked my own life hitch-hiking into a rainforest hundred of miles from home, to visit him.

I snort in disgust and turn and walk away.

All day I walk the Melbourne streets, sweat pouring from my body like rivers pumping from an inner estuary of being. My thoughts confused, swollen. Colours seem too bright and the light is always dazzling.

One thought keeps repeating. One thought is all I need.

I am going to Sydney to see Margarita.

Rocky Horror Show

Novelty wears off

The train ride to Sydney passes in no time. I'd booked a sleeping compartment. I fell asleep after the train left the station. But whereas my slumber from Adelaide to Melbourne had been peaceful, this was one of fast exhausting dreams. In my dreams I was running from an invisible force, a dark stranger. But I couldn't run straight, I kept running round and around in circles, finding myself back at a point I'd started from.

One night the three of us went to see the Rocky Horror Show. Afterwards we drove her home. Falling for her helpless act, and talk of drunks in doorways, he walked her back up to her apartment, leaving me sitting alone in our car. Things would never have gone off the rails between Ray and me if it weren't for her helpless-games. Doing all she could to make me look bad for 'abandoning' her for him and making him feel sorry for her so he felt he had to take care of her.

'Hey, do you want to go and see the Rocky Horror Show?' Margarita asked. Ray and I had run into her by chance at an opening at the Photographers Gallery, in town. It was weeks since I'd moved out of the Castle, moving in with Ray, leaving her there with the big bed of treachery all to herself.

Ray and I had driven into town to look at the new studio. Lily Rosser, Raymond's ex, had been in the crowd at the opening, but she'd left after saying a quick hello.

'I've not seen it,' Margarita continued.

'But it should be good fun. Lots of people get dressed up. It's on in the old art cinema.'

'Yeah it's been running for years,' said Ray. I was surprised to hear him talking seriously about something that seemed to me suburban and banal. The idea bored me, but Ray said, 'Yeah, sure we'll go, sport.' He never ceased to astonish me, but if he wanted to, it was fine by me. We arranged to pick up Margarita the evening after next at the Castle, in our car.

One day Ray and I had walked along the beach from Glenelg to Brighton, walking along the sand. When we reached the jetty he'd pointed to a tall weatherboard building that stood three storeys high above a bait and tackle shop, opposite the pier.

'I've always wanted to live there,' he said.

'Do you still want us to get a place together?'

'Okay,' he replied.

Next day I walked back on my own. Went into the bait and tackle shop, asked an elderly hunch-backed Sicilian woman behind the counter if there were any apartments for rent.

'Yes,' she peered at me with squinting dark eyes, an appraising look. 'There is one, on the third floor.'

The third floor! That would mean with the best views...

'Could I see it?'

She took a set of keys, and without a word led me outside to a door, I followed her up flights of stairs.

The apartment was at the front of the building and running its full width was a sun-room overlooking the Indian Ocean... I gazed out into infinite space, radiant light...curving rim of the world merging into blue sky.

What is Eternity?

It is the sea mixed/ with the sun.[16] A line by Rimbaud ran laughing through my mind.

I skipped over the road, withdrew the deposit from a cash machine, hurried back to give it to my new landlady. It would be the first time I had lived in a rented flat alone with my lover; for four years I had lived with Wolfie in share-houses, as part of economizing, and the way we lived together.

I wanted to be alone with Ray, the two of us, isolated from the public world living in our own world of light, like the first days we were together. Before Margarita arrived.

When we ran into her at the photography opening Margy was acting very upset. She told us that when she returned to the Castle from the Con, the evening before, a drunk man was slumped against the door to her apartment holding a bottle.

Or rather, she told Ray.

I was looking at silver gelatin prints of a lighthouse, as if I didn't care that once again she preferred talking to him rather than me.

'I wasn't sure if he was asleep.'

I found myself listening. She was over-acting putting it on, voice loud with anxiety.

'It was dark as I walked up the stairs. I didn't see him then I did. I almost dropped my violin on him...'

Margarita is timid, I thought. She'd never learned to swim because she was scared of water. I was surprised Ray seemed to be taken in by her 'little girl lost' helpless female act.

My lover was regarding her seriously; looking at her, nodding his head, sympathetically. I couldn't see what all the drama was about. Nothing had happened, she'd just asked the drunk to move away and he had. I didn't say anything, and went to get a refill at the drinks table.

The next night we went to see the Rocky Horror Show in a theatre full of suburbanites dressed in lingerie and gothic make-up. Ray and I drove Margy home. We parked in front of the Haunted Castle looming above. Margy stepped out of the car and closed the door.

Then she leaned into Ray's window on the driver's side, as if a thought just occurred to her.

'I say would either of you two kind chaps care to walk me to my door?' She said in a very English accent she sometimes affected in our younger days.

We put on voices to entertain ourselves. It didn't cover the anxiety in her eyes and smile, doubly nervous, for asking us.

'Go up by yourself, you chicken-livered coward!' I replied in a mock ocker twang, joking.

My hand was on the handle pushing it down, opening the door to go up with her. But before I could, Ray swung around, with a look of fury on his face.

'I'll go up with her,' he hissed. For a moment I was shocked. Until I realized he couldn't be angry, he was joking too.

He jumped out of the car, slammed the door. They walked up the steps together. Margy forgot to say good-bye, but that didn't worry me; we knew each other better than that. I knew she'd be laughing now.

I was still smiling when Ray returned. He was joking too. I'd never known him to be angry. He opened the driver's door. All his movements taut with white-lipped controlled fury.

'I was only jo –' I started to say, but my words cut off as he accelerated, engine roaring, down the street, driving furiously. His eyes fixed ahead. Lips curled together. Face a white mask of rage. I couldn't believe it. What's wrong with him?

He was going too fast. I glanced at the speedometer, quivering at the upper limit. That was not too dangerous in itself not in my old Morris. But Ray's mood was making me nervous. We were driving along a long, straight, flat stretch parallel to the beach, approaching the railway crossing.

'Slow down Ra—,' I put a steadying hand on his forearm.

He shook off my hand and lashed out verbally.

'Just shut up, who do you think you are?'

I don't reply. There is no right answer. Not because it is a rhetorical question but because, suddenly, his body language is frightening, I see the tight fury in his arms, rigid knuckles, gripping onto the steering wheel. The fury of his face set in a mask of anger.

Ray looks like he is impersonating a dangerous maniac. I have an overwhelming urge to burst out laughing, but manage to stop myself just in time.

We fly over the bumpy surface of the level crossing.

He is mad when we park and get out of the car. He is mad as we climb the staircase to our apartment. He is mad, seething, as he turns his key in the front door and we walk in, and he ignores me. He stomps off into the kitchen. As I clean my teeth, I hear him stamping, moving things, and muttering in the living room where he sometimes works. Where he's been trying to work, would be more accurate, in the dining space, connecting the kitchen and bathroom with the balcony room.

Ever since the summer when he failed to complete or really start his masterpiece in his shack in the rainforest, the work of genius locked in his mind, he's continued to try to paint it. Started dozens. Made drawings and thrown them away. He's not getting there. It reminds me of Margarita with her Unfinished Fugue for Three or Four Voices. But whereas she's obsessed with finding a perfect ending, he's trying to create a perfect beginning breakthrough-concept from which his work of genius will grow, nothing else will do. But so far he hasn't found it.

And now it sounds like he's lost it.

Lose your temper and you're a loser, I am tempted to shout through the door, shocked that he is imposing his dark mood in our shared space. But I resist the urge to open the channels of communication. It seems safer to keep quiet.

Suck, roll, and lap. I listen to bay waves crumple onto sand as the street light flickers beneath the window all through the night of rattling cutlery in the kitchen. As he paces kitchen, bathroom, balcony, living room, muttering, and I lie shivering between sheets, suddenly cold.

'I'm going to visit Margarita,' said Ray, early, two days later walking into the balcony-room where I was sitting, writing. I noticed that he had a bottle of wine and his backpack. Right in front of me he held aloft the wine and slid it into the backpack with a flourish.

His manner seemed defiant. But I wasn't worried that he wanted to visit my friend.

No, I thought. It was good that at least one of us was going to visit her. I would rather it were he, I was too busy. I didn't feel guilty that Margarita was left alone in the Castle. She had her violin and she had made it into the Conservatorium. That was taking up her time. She was doing what she wanted now, training to be a violinist. We were twenty-one, I thought. We needed to make our separate lives. She was sure to find a boyfriend of her own soon.

With Ray gone, it meant that I would have the flat to myself, my crystal prism of light. A few more hours in which to play in a sparkling river-rush of thoughts and dreams that I was working into my intricately patterned series on paper. Music pieces. I was trying to paint music.

I looked back at him, thinking: *Don't you know I like to be alone, to paint?*

I turned and watched him open the apartment door.

'You should eat something,' his tone disapproving.

'Okay, Dad.'

He looked at me with his inscrutable blanked-out expression and closed the door behind him.

I was fasting to achieve a state of peace. Two days since I'd eaten. Never had I felt such lightness of being. I was fasting for my art. By leaving me alone Ray was doing me a favour...

But the sharpness of tone, disapproval I heard in his final words, look of displeasure, his face, edges of unpleasantness I thought as I paced the apartment. Yes, hungry. No, will not eat. Yes, breathless, and unsure... No, cannot paint right yet.

I stood looking down onto the beach, watching him walk. I saw a determined figure dressed in blue shorts, blue shirt, straw hat; backpack. He strode along the sand close to the water's edge leaving a double line of footprints.

He walked to the tall sand dunes where the beach curved, and he disappeared. I sat down again at my worktable. Next to me, was an easel with my painting in progress.

I couldn't focus on dream-pieces now.

At the end of the balcony Ray stored some of his things. He had talked of setting up a desk to work on his notebooks.

But that was before I'd set up my table.

At the beginning of the university year I had deferred my course. I thought I would better spend my time developing my painting and writing styles, in our shared prism of light.

Last week he took up a space in a studio in town with the Art Criminals. He went there early, returning after midnight. Drunk, drugged, it was a change. I didn't mind, I liked to be alone, I told myself. I did not have artist's block.

Piles of things left lying around. Folios of his work, visual diaries, propped against the wall, stacks of books on the floor.

I paced. Unable to concentrate I wandered into his side of the sun-room. It felt illicit being in 'his' space with his prisms. I picked one. Held it in front of the window, the light of sky and sea. Watched the rainbows sliding across sharply angled planes through the shining surfaces.

The voice wailed. Brilliant light, dark emotion, and radiant sunshine, I could lose myself in this music. Idly I picked up one of Ray's folders of work.

Ray told me about his projects that resulted in his degree being withheld. I knew about the knife that he stuck through his hand. It was after Lily Rosser left him. He'd come around to the house and shown us the scars.

His hand was swollen three times its normal size, bruised in shocking colours. It looked like a stiff fleshy crab. But there had seemed to be something noble about his gesture, which had been made in the service of Art.

I was holding negatives, contact sheets, of this work.

Raymond's hand stabbed by knife. Dozens of miniature black-and-white frames. And enlarged prints. Feeling rather queasy I turned these over and then paused.

This must be the series Ray told me of with a great cackle.

The Shaving Cuts performance series, where he slashed his face and Tel photographed the art of his self-mutilation.

Rows of images of Ray cutting his face with razor blades. Ray cutting his cheeks, his forehead, chin; blood oozing. His eyes glassy, he looked unwell...ill. Just looking at this work, by myself, without him or anyone else to interpret it, provoked my response untainted by his reputation. I saw it as self-expressive signs of trauma not, as some said as cool indicators of the 'cutting-edge' quality of art, and hipness in the age of self-mutilation art. I felt ill.

I turned to what was underneath:

A large black and white print, three people at a cafe table. Ray sitting in-between a man and a woman I had never seen. She was beautiful with dark wavy hair; gypsy hoop earrings, the man looked muscular, swarthy, wearing a sharp gangster suit. Ray's eyes were huge and glassy as he stared at the camera with an enigmatic smile like a weird underground pin-up boy. He'd laughed about his sedative phase. Was this part of it? Who knew what lay beneath this scene?

I recoiled from the image, all the images.

This wasn't the Ray I knew. But who was the Ray I knew?

I felt shocked, frightened.

It was like seeing a stranger. Suddenly it occurred to me that I didn't really know Raymond Furness at all.

Ray arrived back next night late.

He said that he had stayed in the new studio.

I wanted to talk to Margarita about Ray.

Two days later I caught the bus to Glenelg, we were not on the phone and I hoped she would be in. As I walked up the stairs of the boarding house, I heard her violin play the fugue

I'd heard so many times. I knocked loudly.

'Margy,' I called. 'It's me. Let me in'.

But she didn't open the door.

I went back the next night walked through the backstreets between Brighton and Glenelg not trusting the dark beach.

This time she did open the door.

Metronome

Margarita

16, The Mayfair, 21 December 2001

I was floating through delicious shallows of sleep before waking when the doorbell rang.

Go away, I tell it; I'm not going to answer.

But the ringing doesn't stop. Persistent as a cicada drilling my brain. Whoever it is desperately wants to make contact. I get up reluctantly, head spinning, and walk over to the intercom by the front door.

'Hello?' I run my fingers absently through my spiky hair.

'Margarita?' It can't be. The shock is electric. Suddenly all my senses are on full alert.

'Yes?'

'It's Ruby. Can you let me in?'

Ruby

The Mayfair was one of the city's original art deco buildings, on the corner of a cross street. The door opened. I walked into a well-preserved vestibule with salmon carpet, marble columns, mirror walls and sparkling chandeliers.

An image of the foyer of the Haunted Castle flashed into my mind. Faded men in baggy trousers drifting up and down the stairs like smoking ghosts.

I waited for the lift.

I looked in the mirror, and gasped with horror. Hair thick red with desert dust, eyes wide and slightly wild, cheeks burnt. I looked a lot more dishevelled and feral than I did then.

The doors to the elevator slid open, I stepped in. It's on the sixth floor, she'd said. Number 16.

As I ascended I remembered an anecdote Margy told me when we lived together in the Castle, that brief and highly pressured time. It was when things had started to go bad between us, although I didn't know it, all I knew was she was in a strange mood; treating me with coldness, as if playing with me, which of course with benefit of hindsight, I now know that she was.

She'd been playing violin and was talking to me. I'd asked her what she was playing and she'd not ignored me, dismissed my interruption with a brusque put-down about my musical ignorance that she had begun to specialise in.

She told me about a piece of music, the Unfinished Fugue for Four Voices—that title sticks in my mind. She'd told me about Bach's belief in numerology. He was transcribing the letters of his surname into letter-notes, an air that he was in the process of introducing as a signature third subject into the fugue. Writing himself into his music, which he believed was capable of only being comprehended silently, 'in the mind of God'. But just as he did that, wrote himself into music as it were, he became very ill and died.

'Must have been dangerous music,' I said. 'You'd better be careful...'

She smiled, tossed her black curls over her shoulders, and resumed her eternal practising.

I leaned against the handrail in the lift gripping onto its cool surface. My mind sliding giddily. I stop myself falling. I imagine fugue music swirling around my head. I have a crazy idea that when she opens the door she'll be holding her violin and wearing the black silk slip Mum gave her that she wore all the time.

The lift stops, doors slide, I step onto the sixth floor. Six, what's that in numerology, I wonder. Six, six. I read a numerology book, once. Six, connected to Venus, planet of love, what is the number of the apartment? Sixteen. 6 + 1= 7. Seven. Wasn't that a mystical number?

At the point of attaining self reference, Bach died.

Whoever knows what is going to happen.

I knock, three times.

The door opens.

'Hi'. Cropped hair, wrapped in a red satin robe, Margarita is staring at me in bemusement.

'Rosamond—what's happened? You look as if you've been dragged through a hedge backwards.'

I try to smile. 'I've been in the desert.'

'Which one?'

Margarita always was so particular.

She's standing there holding onto the door as if she could slam it shut.

'Where have you come from?'

'It's a long story. Are you going to let me in?'

We are sitting on the chaise longue. She has made coffee. I have told her that I have been living in London. I've come back for a holiday. She doesn't need to know more than that.

'It's just as well it's Saturday, or I'd be at work even though it's Christmas. I work up until Christmas eve,' she says.

'Work? What do you do?'

'I work in admin. At City University.'

I laugh politely.

Looking around I notice a row of Christmas cards on the book shelf in front of books.

'Your Dad gave me the reference,' she says and laughs.

'I think that's what got me the job!'

'Really?' My mind is reeling.

'What about you. Still painting?'

'Only in my head.'

I gaze towards the windows in buildings across the road. I can see shadowy shapes of people in the opposite windows.

'Have you been following the news?' I ask casually.

'No, I've been trying to cut myself off from the world for a while. That's why I'm here. I'm in recovery,' she says.

No news. Good news. Thank goodness.

I breathe a sigh of relief.

'Recovery from what?' I stare at photos arranged in a large mandala around a geometrical image. I recognize, in surprise, that it is as one of the colour studies Ray used to make.

'The relationship with Raymond,' she says. 'It just got so bad. He treated me badly. He went right off the rails. I can understand why you were scared. You were wise to go when you did.'

You were wise to go when you did.

The fact that my whole life since then has been predicated on that unbearable sense of loss—

??Sheet music with a quick impatient flick of her wrist. Her head tilts at an angle, anchoring the treasured instrument

??????????A???

??d
Margarita is staring at me in bemusement? 'Ruby— what's
happened to you? You look as if
you've
bee??-
???conversation. ?
'Work?
What do you do?? I work in admin at City university, she
says ? ? What
bout?? 4?
????4??
??
??ship with Raymond,"
she
says. It just got bad. He treated me so badly. He went right
off
the rails. I can understand why
you??
??? ???????????????????
???3
223456789101112131
41516171819221222324252626372829303132333435
36373839404142434445464444748495051525354555 65
7585960616263646566676686?????????????????????????????????????
??
??7208209210211 21
2213214215216272182192
2022122222322422522622722822923023123223323 4
23523623723823924024124224324424524624724828249
2??
??

210

???????????????????????????of the Southern Spiral hotel group—
even though he's
   chosen to live in, he went to Yarrow so I
   feel
   I???
   ???
   ??????????????she was   Fears and demands and threats—who
will ever
   Kno???
   ???
   ???????????????know
   What she was doing! ? ?   'Well, doesn't that say it all,'
said

She is sitting close to me. The sweet smell of her perfume
is making me feel queasy. I look around at the airy room with
its polished floorboards, contemporary furniture.
   'It looks like you've done well,' I say.
   She's done very well, I think. Despite what she says about
'abuse.'
   'Rosamond,' she says changing the subject. 'You look like
you need a shower, would you like one?'
   'I'd love a shower'.
   It must be six days since I had a shower. At the Southern
Spiral Hotel with Hugo the day that I found Ray.
   An eternity separates me from that time, as nebulous and
definite as the boundary between two worlds.
   'This way,' she says standing up, opening a door.

The water jet cascades over my head, neck, shoulders, back.
It washes off dust, sweat, grime but it doesn't wash away the

tension which is increasing the longer I'm in her flat.

I turn off the water, step from the shower and wrap myself in white fluffy towels she left for me. I dry my hair. An image of blue and white striped towels in the ensuite of Hugo's and my bedroom in Rivers Chase flashes to mind. That seemed unreal. This is my life.

The real life of the real Ruby.

Scorned point of triangle Raymond-Ruby-Margarita. But what she had said about 'abuse' doesn't quite fit with what he said of Margarita as his 'best friend.' Was she lying; was he? When my hair is almost dry, I walk out into the living room.

'How do you feel?' She is looking at me very intently.

'I'm really tired actually.'

'Why don't you rest, sleep in my bed? Borrow my clothes. I'll put your things in the washing machine.'

She gets up and walks past me, brushing against me.

I follow her. Past the bathroom up a small flight of stairs. We walk towards our reflections in a mirror on a small landing. I watch our ascension. First Margarita then me. We turn, walk up another flight of stairs. She leads me to her bedroom.

I notice a painted Mexican wardrobe next to the bed, on top of it, an old metronome. The room is tidy, clean, light and airy. I can't connect it with the Margarita I used to know.

I lie down on the bed still wrapped in a towel.

She lies down next to me.

'Rosamond.' She says my name like it's a statement. I can feel her looking at me.

'Margarita?'

'Yes?'

'Do you still play the fugues you played when we were living together in the Haunted Castle?'

'Bach's fugues, do you mean?'

'The Unfinished Fugue.'

'You remembered!' She sounds surprised.

'I stopped playing. Raymond wouldn't let me practice in the house. I had to practice down the road in a church hall. I graduated then stopped playing.'

'I've got Bach's *Art of Fugue* on CD,' she says. 'I can put that on. I often listen to it as I'm going to sleep. It's my bedtime music,' she adds. I recoil inwardly at her tone.

She leans over to the player beside her bed.

Haunting bars drift quivering through the air. The searing clean profound beauty of a violin solo.

Young woman alone
Playing violin
Falling Dusk
Darkening Room

She half sits and leans over me. The top of her Japanese robe falls open. Her breasts are pale lilies floating on a dark pond.

She leans down and kisses my mouth. 'I've got Bach's Art of Fugue,' she says. I can put that on. I often listen to as I'm going to sleep...It's my bedtime music'. She leans and touches the player beside her bed.

The first slow haunting bars of the fugue, the searing profound beauty of a solo violin shatters the still warm air...

The last thing I want to feel is her body wrapped around me. I wanted Raymond, or had wanted Raymond, love of my life. The love she stole away from me.

'Ruby I always wanted you,' she says, stroking my hair.

She calls me by my *nom de art*. Puts her mouth to mine. Her hands on my shoulders, torso. I'm crushed by her body's perfumed weight. I'm beneath her, legs hitting the wardrobe, trying to gain a footing—

Suddenly there is an explosion.

Everything goes red, magenta, crashing cerise, ruby red—

Spilling, splashing, over sheets, and dripping and gushing onto polished floorboards of the immaculate designer home interior.

Raymond

Margarita didn't answer. I was taking out my key. Then after my ringing, the intercom crackled and a voice said:

'Hello?'

'Who's that?' I asked.

'Raymond! It's Ruby. Ruby red, ruby love, ruby Monday— do you want to come up to my ruby world of ruby joy?'

'What are you are on?'

Usually it was me doing the slurring. I don't much like to see a woman in that state. There was no reply.

The doors opened. I sauntered through the lobby. Pressed for the lift. Ascended to the level of rich and successful at an even speed.

I walked down the corridor to number 16, knowing something was amiss. But I didn't know how out of it she was.

I knocked on the door.

It opened slowly.

She must have been standing there. Waiting for me.

Naked. Covered in blood.

'Holding Margarita's metronome.'

Hugo

'Doesn't that say it all,' said Jed Finke-Burton.'Mince pie?'

'I maintain she was under duress, brainwashed. He took her into the desert! He made her take drugs—intimidated her—fears, demands, threats—who knows what happened there? It said in the medical report she was confused, disoriented—she didn't know what she was doing!' Jed said.

I delicately nibbled the little pie.

'I'm trying for a retrial. She is innocent, of course, sweetly innocent. But that judge, and jury, the fools could not see the remorseless red-headed ruffian was to blame, not Ruby. Not my Ruby. She was set up.'

I was sitting over room service with Finke-Burton owner of Southern Spiral hotel group. Even though he's chosen to live here, he went to Yarrow. I can trust him. And he's become a pillar to me in this time.

First Ruby's disappearance, reappearance, and now this.

'It is obvious that she was intimidated and pressured to go into the desert,' said Finke-Burton. 'He wanted Margarita killed, using undoubtedly skilful techniques of persuasion, which made it possible to abduct Ruby in the first place, no doubt persuaded her to do it.'

I didn't quite catch what he was saying.

'The abducted are said to fall in love with the abductor, it's a form of defence. You heard of that heiress—kidnapped and brainwashed then freed to return to the bosom of her family and become her self again,' he continued.

'My wife equally needs a chance for justice and I will not

215

let this matter drop.'

The Mistress Departs and takes her Fake-Furs
Professor's Wife Condemned to Life in an Australian Jail

What to say, to think? When one's whole life is turned upside down?

An anecdote I use sometimes in First Year Epistemology. Until the settlement of Australia it was believed that swans were white. Black swans were then discovered in Australia. What does this say about the nature of knowledge? Belief? What kind of belief was that?

Ruby, my black swan sailing gracefully down a river from my heart, on a journey I cannot follow.

The last thing I said to her as they led her away was: 'Keep up with your reading!'

Poor girl, I tried to be encouraging.

Her eyes I remember flashing, proud, were hollow circles. But I still see my wife as mysterious, desirable, commanding, yet biddable—Damn what they say. What do press-parasites know about love?

Ruby. My wife.

But not anymore—it seems now—my life.

What I will not ever think about is the trial, her testimony.

The hysterical talk she came out with.

That crazy talk about that ruffian who abducted her.

Even worse about her best friend. Not that I have anything intrinsically against such feeling. It is part of research for my book, which is almost complete. I've moved on. My assistant would be so pleased I finished that chapter. She was right it was all 'so nineteenth century.'

But what she said at the Trial makes me convinced that the real criminal put fabricated nonsense into her mind.

That was not my Ruby speaking.

My Ruby belonged to me. And me only.

When I return I shall hire a good defence lawyer—I shall not rest until we have a re-trial. I need her back. Have to have her back.

The images of her will not desist, teasing and tormenting me with excruciatingly sweet hope of eventual reunion, more than a hope, it must be a promise.

Though it may take a while to become used to Rosamond. ??? ??????????????4??? ??//of the Southern hotel group—even though he's chosen to live in this colony, he went to Yarrow so I feel

I?? ??? ?????????????know what she was doing! ?   ? Doesn't that say it all, said Finke-Burton, 'mince pie?'

4??

Rivers Chase, Charnot Square, 5 March, 2003

I rest the file folder on the surface of the ladies writing desk in the old mistress bedroom so named for reasons of the house's history; it was Ruby's former retreat. I pause for a moment, staring through the window at the pre-dawn autumn mist swirling eerily through Primrose Hill.

I suck on my post-breakfast cigarette and wonder if recent phenomena such as 'repressed memory syndrome,' 'taken by aliens' claims can in truth be seen as 'less dramatic, more subtle signs of distress,' than Victorian vapours, swoons, trances,

217

fits and fugues, which were epidemics in nineteenth century Europe.

All were seen as attention seeking behaviours, hysterical, none subtle...I pour another nip of scotch from the engraved silver hip flask, Ruby's gift which since her departure, I have kept close at all times. I take a swig, gazing out into the dawn fog. Ranulph Thimpson applied the terms 'dissociation state,' and 'drug-induced', to describe her, in her defence.

I appreciate any points that could be made in my darling's favour. This reduced first-degree murder to manslaughter due to 'diminished responsibility.'

Phuff. Not Ruby.

That my wife be charged with diminished responsibility is a ludicrous joke. Ruby was superbly, regally, in control.

But, must not speak of her; think of her in the past tense. Two years apart is nothing. Self-control is all. Oddly enough my research prepared me for difficult times. The practice of disavowal, deferred gratification, discipline, is what develops conscience (Freud pointed out) but it also steels one to cope with the vicissitudes of life.

Her sense of responsibility and duty as she went about her business remains forever in my mind...

Still, it is obvious to me the scoundrel Furness is responsible; that is what we are pursuing in campaign for a re-trial. Evidence has come to light that Furness was in the apartment earlier. He might have taken her there. A cleaner witnessed them in the building; it's sufficient evidence for a re-trial.

'Tis pity law needs such extensively proven motives to prove his action when Ruby was locked up so quickly. To me it's obvious he was driven to jealous rage because Margarita, whom he loved had been re-united with Ruby. Obviously he took Ruby to the Mayfair apartment thinking they would be alone. Ruby and Margarita were best friends, it seems more than friends; or at least Margarita wanted it that way. When he saw that it drove him into an uncontrollable rage.

Ruby-Rosa

Newcastle Jail, August 2003

*Repetition...Distortion...Elaboration...Mirroring...*Margarita's words echo...*Diminution...Inversion...* Her voice comes back at odd points throughout the day and night as I go through the motions of regular pre-determined routine. It's all laid out for me. All that is required from me now, in this life, is for me to make of my being an entity akin to the rhythmic hands of a pre-wound clock.

There is little requirement for sudden movement, changes in tempo, required to be accurate, uncomplaining cog. My set hours—my programs—don't change.

Not like Margarita's metronome.

Sometimes images flash into thoughts of Margarita's metronome. I imagine it, swinging wildly, out of control, as our bodies wrestle together on the bed, sickening crash of it—the dull thud—as the heavy triangular object smashed down. She fell from the bed onto the floor. And I am beside her, as she is falling sliding in slow motion, again, in my thoughts, my eyes splashed by blood, spurting with astonishing force—suddenly—all over her face, my face.

My hands wet with blood clasping the metronome, blood. I didn't know what I was doing. I told the judge, numb with disbelief and grief.

What I should have said, meant to say but the words came

out wrong was: I don't know what I did.

Did the metronome fall dislodged as they wrestled on the bed? Hitting her face and head? Did she reach up? Had she—
Your Honour, the wardrobe was too high for her to reach it.

All is a blur, dizzy spinning rush of colours, heat and pain.
Blood kept flowing all over me.
I was frozen. Don't know how long. Doorbell rang.
It kept ringing and ringing.
I woke. Forced me awake and wrapped in a bloody sheet.
Stumbled down stairs, through the apartment.
'Yes?' I spoke into the intercom.
Such a terrible pain, my head.
I opened the front door.

Calling Paintings into Being

Young woman alone
Playing violin
Falling dusk
A darkening room

Newcastle Jail. New South Wales

I pick up brush and palette knife, paint slow, neat strokes, dabbing at silver, grey, blue, colours merge into outlines of she who I see deep in my inner eye.

Her face trembles in an expression of sweet intense private pain she gives herself up to, when she believes herself unseen. Acute aesthetic anguish inherited from her grandfather, a solo violinist in the Berlin Philharmonic, until SS herded him onto the train to the concentration camp, and crushed his knuckles. He survived and emigrated to Australia.

I hover in the shadows of the doors, in the kitchenette in the balcony-room, like a dark-eyed oblique-looking girl in a painting by Paula Rego. Family girls who always seem to be caught up in some obscure project of their own seem to strike a chord with her.

I hold my breath but she doesn't give any indication she's noticed me. She's too far gone, soaring on high-pitched ribbons of sound. Intense folds swirling violently through the gloom.

What is she playing, something by Bach, one of his fugues. 'Bach was the master of the art of fugue,' she told me. When she wasn't playing she talked about the music, told me many stories. Lecturing me with an air of superior authority which always secretly amused me.

'Labyrinths fascinated baroque composers. Mazes, mirrors…they attempted to find infinity in their music.

'Surely, you mean an illusion of infinity?' I interject. She has paused and I now join her in the warmth and light of the last sunbeam slanting through the French doors.

'That's all the knowledge we have of it anyway,' she retorts. I smile. We have been arguing about illusion, reality, qualities of matter, non-matter, material and immaterial objects since we did quantum mechanics at Randolph Sterner School.

We had first met in a class on digital imaging; together we made an amusing monster.

'In some of Bach's later mirror fugues notes on bars appear to mirror ad infinitum, and that's apart from the potentially infinite circularity of fugue, which is ended by the composer with a cadence. Is infinity an illusion, or do number patterns repeat forever, and what does 'forever' mean?'

Hold infinity in the palm of your hand. I quote, teasingly.

And eternity in an hour.[17] She can't mistake Blake. Quoting poets at each other, line by line, is a favourite game of ours.

It is found again! I continue.

What? She says, obligingly, if unwittingly…

Eternity/It is the sea mixed/With the sun.[18] Rimbaud. I finish the quatrain gazing at her, willing her to 'Smile'! She looks at me crossly and returns to her obsession.

'In a fugue subject melodies are played by different voices or instruments in many variations. The theme is distorted, embellished, mirrored, inverted, diminished, in counterpoint.

'All I know about the subject,' I contribute, 'is that a 'fugue' is a psychological condition of amnestic block, memory loss. There was an article about it in the *Mirror*; an Adelaide lawyer disappeared when on a fishing trip. His wife and children were desperate. He turned up at a police station, hundreds of kilometres away, weeks later, he'd lost his memory of himself, didn't know who he was. It's a form of amnesia.'

I didn't know a fugue was also a type of music.'

'You wouldn't. You're such a musical philistine.'

She tartly enunciates the words, picks up a lump of rosin, rubs it up and down the length of the horsehair bow, glancing at me then deliberately looking away.

The 'seductive put-down'. Part of her playful style.

Then she returns to infinity.

'Bach's mirror fugues apparently were in his words, or in their translation from German, pieces of 'sublime music,' designed to be only fully comprehended in 'the mind of God.' (Or the reader-God). When you read the music the notations in parallel bars appear to repeat well, infinitely... It's an effect you only 'get' if you're reading the music, you can't hear it, except in your mind.'[19]

She talks about numerology and Bach's Unfinished Fugue from Three (or Four) Voices, or subjects, melody lines. 'Bach was writing the fugue when he died. He'd translated the letters of his name using gematria, the number alphabet into a melody, each letter corresponding to note: B—A—C—H. (H is B sharp in German). He was writing his signature, coded name, as a third subject line into the piece, *Fuga a Soggetti* or *Contrapunctus 14*, when he had a stroke and went blind. Shortly after he died. Imagine that...

Carl Philipp Emanuel Bach, his son, wrote on the manuscript that while his father was working on this fugue, where his name BACH is introduced as a countersubject, the author died.[20]

Scholars argue that the fourth 'voice' or melody line, was the Art of Fugue subject line, and some scholars have tried to 'complete' it, such as Tovey in 1931. In a rendition by Tovey he made a new mirror fugue on four subjects from the unfinished fugue.'[21]

Her soprano voice soars with enthusiasm.

'It was as if in attaining self-reference Bach literally wrote himself out of this world, into the 'mind of God', as he might have seen it, transcending from life to the after-life...'

'Repeating to infinity?' I ask, unable to resist teasing her just a little bit more. 'How sublime, darling!'

She hits a discordant note. Her violin screeches in protest.

'It's not funny,' she says, shooting me a pained look.

??? ??n. An intellectual mind-game. Baroque composers were fascinated by

labyrinthine effects: mazes, mirrors...They were??????-??together. Is the notion of 'infinity' illusion or can certain immaterial things, number patterns, like certain musical

??? ??? ??????

?????????????????????????????????//////???????????????????????????? ???in

the *Mirror* last week. In a fugue a person forgets who they are, they lose awareness of their

??
??
??art, picks
up the lump of rosin and rubs it up and down the quivering
length of the her bow's horsehair, very slowly and

??
??
???

Bach was writing the fugue when he died. He'd translated
the letters of his name into a countersubject

??
??
?????????????????????s// *'It's not funny,'* she says, *shooting me a pained
look.*

/// *The Unfinished*

??
?????????????????

I hear it even here, even now. Margarita's music. I can't stop
hearing it. Can't push a button, turn it off. Twisting and turning around my head, screeching, echoing, crashing. A ghostly
fugue that never stopped, never stops. She was preparing to
audition for the Conservatorium. She practiced all day, at
night. Shimmering like an apparition, a vision, in the shadows of the haunted castle. Her practice never-ending practice.
Driving me away.

Oh, here it comes, high-pitched music—her pain, sadness
striving towards beauty, which I could not take seriously. Yes,
what I failed to consider, I didn't take Margy seriously, never
reckoned on her force. My 'satellite personality' as Raymond
called her 'charmingly,' aptly I was happy to think, in the first
crystal days—when she arrived, with her violin in hand: 'Sur-

prise, I've come to stay!' In the early days of summer. That hot and crazy time.

Our only summer.

???
?????????n. An intellectual

mind-game. Labyrinthine affects fascinated baroque composers: mazes, mirrors…they were

att???
???
?? together. Is the notion of

'Infinity' illusion, or can certain immaterial things, like number patterns, like certain musical

??
??
?????????????????

in the Mirror. In a state of fugue a person forgets who they are, they lose awareness of their

??
??
???art, picks up the lump of rosin

and rubs it up and down the quivering length of her bow's horsehair, very slowly and

??
??????????????????was in the process of writing

the fugue when He'd translated the letters of his name, into a subject—

??
??
??

226

??????? ? 'It's not funny,' shooting me a pained look ???   The Unfinished
???
??????????????

Margarita—will not—mention Margarita my best friend must not mention MARGARITA!

Deep breath down calm down RELAX! Paper bag over the head what a muted thrill-spill   sliding down the hill

Shift attention from missing facts.

Shying away from the long-lost reality, the vanished truth of banished moments I'm trying to conjure, hold within the eye of memory paint. Translate into colours and form of material reality, She who was my best friend. Turn her into an object of art. To hang upon a stranger's wall.

Have to go deeper; remember Margarita as she really was, as I saw her once, many times, when long ago we lived together, I have to bring back and paint the images that I hope will lead me, tap-tap-tap, towards full conscious recall, diver about to descend into murky water.

The institution greens (mint; pea) and chalk-dust smell of E-Room, papier-mâché platters, Chatterton, and the security guard at the door; all disappear.

Shimmering time and space. A ghost, apparition, vision. She is quivering in rapt concentration, herself an instrument, in the patch of half-light in the room. Beside the 1940's dark varnished table which I think should be my desk. On it are my abandoned things. Books, papers, essay drafts, drift.

I am standing in a narrow kitchen in the one-room apartment with a glassed-in balcony kitchen. The floor slopes at a slight but alarming angle, it felt like if you jumped the room would fall crashing into the overgrown garden below.

Everything is miniature, doll-size, in the balcony-room. A card-table, one-ring gas stove, bar-fridge. Concealed behind a threadbare yellow curtain and built into the wall is a shelf-bed like the beds in traditional nineteenth-century European gypsy caravans. She pulls her knees up to fit onto it. So: there is a double bed in a room with no windows but French doors open onto the balcony turned into a little room with kitchen facilities and a tiny bed behind a curtain.

It was the only place we could find after arriving, spending hours walking in the late-February heat through labyrinthine streets behind the Glenelg beach. We had moved to Adelaide together. I was returning to university, second year. Margarita had dropped out of her course in Melbourne, hoping to study violin at the Conservatorium. I had brought my typewriter, books, and paints; she had brought her violin.

We tossed a coin. Margarita lost. My lucky 'tails' won the room furnished with an ancient sagging double bed made up on arrival with yellowed sheets and grey army blanket. (That I replaced with my sleeping bag). A wardrobe loomed almost to the ceiling, at the end of the double bed.

'It looks like the wardrobe in *The Renter*' Margarita sniffed.

After that, images from the noir classic flashed recurrently through my mind. I saw a closet transsexual in gothic make-up hiding inside its interior, biding time, waiting to leap out when we least expected. As I fell asleep every night, I turned from the wardrobe holding our clothes all mixed up together.

The table in the big room matched the wardrobe from the 1940s made of solid wood coated with dark varnish.

I imagined myself arranging writing things, books, easel, a studio. The evening we moved in Margy started practicing.

'Can't you play in the kitchen?' I asked. She curled her lip in an expression of ravishing contempt. I thought she looked like a classical violinist in this mien. I listened to her politely.

'What are you talking about?' she hissed. I looked at her. Standing, head thrown back, full lips quivering.

'I can't play in the kitchen. There's no room in the kitchen. Why can you not take this seriously?' Her high-pitched voice rose until it was ringing almost hysterically, in my ears.

I looked at her in more concern. I knew how important this was. I thought about her grandfather. Her grandmother, murdered in a camp. Ghosts trembled in the air between us. And at that moment nothing seemed more important than Margy playing her violin. The Minsk family instrument.

'Okay, then,' I said. 'That's fine.'

For weeks I had not written or painted in the apartment. My assignments were gathering dust on the table behind her metronome. But I kept my anxiety to myself. I didn't want to upset her.

Carefully, I slide the palette knife along the length of her pale arms, rolling in streaks of white to make a luminescence. Painting from memory, I stroke outlines. Her high forehead. Lines of her features quivering with the refinement and complexity of the music. She told me it was 'Baroque' as opposed to 'classical.' But it was all the same to me.

The music I liked was punk, new-wave, post-punk rock 'n' roll. Patti Smith, Joy Division, Boys Next Door... Not that I was getting much chance to play my music, I consoled myself with the thought that at least one of us wasn't taking out a retirement pension at age twenty-one, at least one of us was still in touch with the modern world. And it wasn't my best friend.

Margarita had recently renounced her electric violin. Her music. I thought her music was brilliant. Improvised manic mazurkas she played with her band Deconstruction. I danced in nightclubs. I went busking with her in improvised performances of a doll on inner city streets and in public squares. We performed together in art galleries, car parks, in shopping malls.

She had photographed my dramatizations of my poems and performances, later she used these for her college assignments. Using my poems though she omitted to acknowledge me as author. In one of her last assignments she used photographs of my dramatization of my poem.

I lost myself today at tea between the bread and jam/and now I wander round the house and don't know who I am.[22]

Which ended with me, naked, on an office chair.

Her lecturer had asked her who wrote that poem, and she said her friend (me), who was also the 'model' and the art director/designer, her lecturer said she had to acknowledge me, it was her friend's (my) piece. She did all of her assignments for that subject this way, using my written works.

I did not think much about it at the time (though I wasn't too happy she was using my original works I'd become used to it, there was always a culture of being kind, helping Margy in our family). It was only with this poem-image at the end of her first year that her lecturers started to ask what was she doing, where were the writings from that she was basing her photos on, saying to her that it wasn't her own original work. There were hints of integrity being breached. Plagiarism as she hadn't attributed the author, poet and designer. That's when she first mentioned it to me, decided to quit her course and leave Melbourne.

I couldn't understand why she'd chosen to give up her own art: the music that came from her heart and soul. To train for the ranks of classical musicians in an orchestra.

'Margy, could you please take a break, I need to work on an essay. I'd also like to listen to something else for once.'

'Rosamond, I've told you; I've got to get this right for my audition. No. I can't stop.'

'Okay then, I'm going out.' Slam!

As the days passed we were becoming locked in a silent— or non-verbalized—battle. Disquiet splintered between us on discords and squeaks.

After three weeks I was in danger of fails for my subjects at university. I could not concentrate on writing with her violin taking over my space and life. Ironically Margy was taking a media art elective that I enrolled in. She had been accepted at the Con and was allowed to take subjects at other universities. I deferred, withdrew from the course, but she stayed in the art and politics subject that I had told her about and wanted to do.

I found the apartment with Ray. I worked on my writing, in blissful quiet, overlooking the Indian Ocean. Ray went out every day to the Criminals' studio. I sensed, then found out, that she had moved in on my love. Well, why not? She had entered every other area of my life. It should have come as no great surprise.

Transgression was the fashion. It was banal and bourgeois to care. I was way out of fashion.

Her eyes iridescent blue, fringed with black curling lashes. 'I have my mother's Irish eyes,' she said once. I thought that a bit gruesome, her mother died in an accident when Margy was three. Azure. Add a touch of white to lighten it a bit. Then I stroke in her eyelashes with the tip of my sable brush (sent by Hugo). Her nose is straight, a noble nose.

And then, heart pounding, I dip the knife in the cadmium and pink. Mix, test, and approach the canvas.

I have plenty of time to paint and do research here. Ironic that in all the years in London I ran Ruby Gallery (my own gallery!), I didn't even doodle.

I borrow books from the prison library, five each fortnight. I order in books through the library, linked to the library network. I'm allowed to keep a small collection of my books in the cell. Every morning after my breakfast of porridge, juice, and coffee, followed by fifty laps walk of the walled perimeter—I do my research.

I sit on bed leaning against the flat prison pillow, which I prop against the wall behind my back. Before I start my work I glance up at the clock bolted onto the wall.

10.45 a.m., precisely. Every morning since transfer here, it's been the time I start my research, with minor variations of the clock's minute hand. 10.43; 10.46. The most exciting thing that happens here all day is the movement of the hands around that clock face.

I've developed a routine. Self-disciplined study habits to stop me going crazy here. Painting in the afternoon, now they let me paint. With the small rather philistine kind of satisfaction you get from sticking to a plan and starting to see results, I pick up *History of European Art*. It's my own book. Hugo gave it to me before he left. The second time. That was before I was transferred here from Sydney.

'Something to inspire and soothe your soul, darling.'

He gave me a gift wrapped in pink paper covered with images of cherubs.

Hugo could always be relied upon for an elevated turn of phrase and had a knack for choosing an unlikely gift. Things that if you thought about it you probably always wanted.

My husband. He is still on my side against the accusers. Margarita's colleagues and so-called 'evidence' they made up.

He reassures me in frequent letters and mails that he still believes in me. *'Venus! My Boadicea!'* His voice booms when I read his words. Like the foghorn of a safe ship sailing away leaving me incarcerated in the Hunter Valley.

Hugo wanted me to intentionally play the part of his Ideal Woman. But I accidentally became Lady Macbeth. Eternally washing hands. Cadmium blood stains snow-white skin. Red paint drips off the canvas onto the floor.

No one visits me in jail.

Everyone thinks I did it, except Hugo. The gang of people whom Margarita worked with gave their fabricated evidence and false allegations, mendacious accusations claiming Margarita said the things about me they said in court: that she said I was violent and abusive, they used evidence that there was a rift, I had been kicked out of my family because I was unfairly accused of being a 'rebel', my parents didn't like Wolfie (son of one of Dad's colleagues whom they all seemed to know). Then they said damaging things about my marriage to Hugo. Z, a supposed friend of Margarita's, said that Margy said to her that I liked to inflict violence.

Nothing could be further from truth. I did not care for the research. It was a trial, which I did out of wifely duty. They even insinuated that I broke Hugo's arm!! He was knocked off his bike when cycling. That was thrown out when the doctor who hit Hugo off his bike then patched up his arm gave a statement. And how could they claim such things when I had not seen, nor spoken to, Margarita for years? It seemed they could invent and say what they liked; they did their 'research' and they fabricated their story.

They said that I was an 'unreliable narrator'.

My mother and brother do not visit. Ray lives in Sydney, he has not visited me or been in touch.

There is no such a thing as a 'private life' any longer, I tried to tell Hugo, he ignored me. Sade was jailed, the 'libertines' in *One Hundred and Twenty Days of Sodom* raped, tortured, murdered women-philosophers. Hugo explained this horror was a critique of oppression in decadent Ancient Regime culture. I thought that symbolically it continued it.

Yet I ended up in jail for something I did not do.

Hugo pointed out that Sade had not done anything more heinous than write about the excesses and decadence of the society he lived in, and he 'really' was a supporter of women. Yet his work was unpopular (was that surprising I thought?) Unlike the works of the novelist from whom sexual pathology of 'masochism' takes its name who had a devoted readership across nineteenth-century Europe. *Venus in Furs* by history professor, nobleman, Leopold von Sacher-Masoch, fictionalised his search for fulfilment, enacting a desire for a woman in furs by a submissive male protagonist who worshipped her. It was an 'alternative' form of relationship to the conventional marriage of the time, and meant to be a search for meaning and intense romantic love. Many women (and men) wrote

234

to Masoch offering to play the character and the woman who became Masoch's wife changed her own name to that of the novel's dominatrix: Wanda von Dunajew. In reality she struggled in this according to letters. She did not fulfil the role; Masoch continued seeking his fantasies of the roles that obsessed him (including 'the Greek' a male, in a triangular relationship).[23] I imagine in real life she was not an Ideal Woman, unrealistic object of desire, but a real woman.

She was according to accounts, pilloried and attacked, and accused of violence against Masoch for playing the very role prescribed in her husband's books. By playing object of desire women are thus oppressed. And the social realm of masochism can be oppressive, suffocating. If I had known when I found Hugo's advertisement I would not have suggested I play that part. There can be nothing more mendacious, as it feeds the power-complex of women's oppressors, than the idea that women achieve 'liberation' through role-playing the dominatrix or, even worse, by 'allowing' themselves to be subjugated or beaten, which is a practice of violent and dangerous oppression, by the time they realize this, it may be too late.

For myself, jailed for a crime I did not commit, a murder that I did not do, lies fabricated against me by liars who cited my relationship with Hugo as so-called 'evidence' I am 'violent' and a 'sadistic' woman. If it had been the other way around, if he had wanted to role-play that part and I had gone along with it, I would have been accused of enjoying my oppression and blamed for that. I despair.

I tried to convince Hugo, that masochism (let alone sadism) was a construct that oppresses women who participate or become involved in it, tried to lead him to other things, but he was stuck.

Now it is me who is stuck in this blasted jail—for life.

I received Hugo's letter from London last week. Brought to me by Jackson, the Sydney dealer he's appointed to show and sell my 'prison paintings.' 'You've become famous.'

He reads a headline.

MURDERER-ART DEALER SHOW SELLS OUT

Did he think I'd be pleased by this news; I would be ecstatic to hear about my so-called 'success' as an artist? At such a cost?

As if that means anything here. The art world that I loved. A million years ago in London. Crime of passion. A French defence. Turned into stories, for the next generation of falling joys.

It was to be faithful to Margarita's obsession that I chose to paint a series of portraits of her in a new style using elements that characterized Baroque in painting.

A fascination with illumination; juxtaposition of high and low; people's everyday life never depicted as the subject of high art before; ordinary, low-life characters radically illuminated by divine light; a fascination with tricks, labyrinths, mazes, infinity. But the defining feature of art of the Baroque was what was left out of frame, unstated, the unseen presence to which figures turn; the out-of-frame source of a brilliant ray of light illuminating barefoot tavern drinkers, like Caravaggio's painting, *The Calling of St Matthew.*

What was out of frame? What was it that I couldn't see? In that tangled intense time the three of us spent together.
??

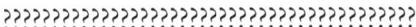

That never stopped. She was preparing to audition for the Adelaide Conservatorium. She
??
????????????????? 'satellite personality' isn't that what
Raymond called her, charmingly, yet aptly, I was happy to think, in those first crystal days—when she
???

The page I want is book-marked by photographs. Margarita and Raymond and I at the Farm. It is mid-summer in the land of the high country.

Ray and Margy laughing at their long-forgotten joke. They are glowing in the full glare of the sun as if they've been irradiated. They look as if they are haloed by light. But I don't want to look at them now.

I turn to what is on the page, in the History of Art.

The Maids of Honour (Las Meninas) 1656
Diego Velázquez (1599-1660)
Oil on canvas 10' x 5"x 9'

I look at Velázquez's work. It takes up a whole page. It's grey, black and white; its wash of greys is grainy. But magic shimmers off the page. The image, saturated with forms of light, dances into my eyes. Princess Margarita with blonde fluffy hair, surrounded by playmates and maids, a dwarf and loose-jowelled Flemish dog. To her left and right, girls curtsey in displays of avid attendance. The group is standing in a studio room where the viewer assumes Princess Margarita has just been posing or is about to. Velázquez, the artist, painted himself, a long-haired moustachioed figure holding palette and brush. Standing before a canvas the height of the room. Its edge is visible to the left side of the canvas, as if propped inside the painting, itself.

Two smaller figures are reflected in a mirror on the wall at the end of the room. Historical research reveals they are Princess Margarita's royal parents, but it is impossible to tell this from the blurry indistinct image alone.

Whether their images are a reflection of images Velázquez has painted on the canvas or reflections of the couple out-of-frame in the space where the viewer is positioned, to which the group in the portrait is looking towards the implied viewer gazing into the portrait, is unknown. The painting is a stage with the fourth wall removed, for the viewer to look into.

Beside the mirror is a doorway at the top of a small flight of stairs, where stands a male figure. The stairs lead up into a rectangle of brilliant light, at the vanishing point. This figure is turned towards the viewer.

Looking back at the viewer looking forwards.

Although it was painted two hundred years before photography's advent it looks as if all the figures are turning to a photographer who has captured them as they turn before a formal pose is struck.

Velázquez opened a window onto a visible world created from light, challenging the viewer in the process to enter his mirror-world labyrinth of reflections and optical tricks. What at first sight appears to be a straightforward group portrait is revealed on closer view to be a complex maze of shimmering mirage-meaning...

I have gazed long and hard into this image and yet have not come closer to solving the mysteries and paradoxes it sets up. There's always more I have to do. More pictures to paint. Can't stop now.

At night in dreams, she whispers softly brusquely, telling me about fugues... Their structure, content, history, genesis... My ear tickles with her spectral breath, the cell echoes to the sound of her fugal violin. In my dreams she is standing in the room. Dressed in Mother's black silk slip, playing the unfinished fugue for three or four voices, our voices, the music that once drove me crazy.

I see her in my mind. I can look at her, but I cannot touch her, cannot reach her. I can paint her but cannot make her look at me, cannot make her smile, talk. No matter how many pictures I might paint and words I may write, I cannot make the words return.

I cannot make the blood flow back.

I cannot give her life.

Coda

Cockle Beach House, Sydney

It's six weeks since the real murderer confessed. I have been released. George worked with Margarita, came home early from his overseas deployment and let himself in to the apartment he owned. I still can't recall anything that happened because he hit me on the head as well as Margarita. It turned out he was in love with her and wanted to marry her. He missed her, and cut his leave short wanting to surprise her. He let himself in; we couldn't hear that because of the loud music. But he walked into the bedroom, saw us, went mad, attacked us both hitting us with ceramic plates he brought back from Portugal to give her. He cleaned up the plates, left. Raymond arrived; I was accused, prosecuted, tried, convicted; 'branded,' victim of prejudice and hateful allegations. By people George and Margarita had both worked with at City University.

A large amount of compensation will be awarded to me soon but it cannot make up for years in jail. I've been trying to process what happened through writing and art. I needed to be alone for a while after I was released

I'm in Sydney although I will leave soon. Fly back to my life in London. I'm staying at the beach in the holiday house of a family friend. I write at night 'til the hours before dawn that some call small hours, which I think of as the large hours as time seems to expand then. I write with a view of the South Pacific Ocean; the crying of seagulls is the music of daytime, at night, silence and the laptop keys ring in my ears.

You can't remember committing a murder if you didn't do it, but you can try to imagine it in writing.

I'm almost at peace now.

The voices have ceased.

It takes a while to become used to justice, believe I am free.

List of Works

Untitled 1, 2019 digital photomedia, pixel abstract
Untitled 2, 2019 digital photomedia, pixel abstract
Untitled 3, 2019 digital photomedia, pixel abstract
Untitled 4, 2019 digital photomedia, pixel abstract
Untitled 5, 2019 digital photomedia, pixel abstract
Untitled 6, 2019 digital photomedia, pixel abstract
Untitled 7, 2019 digital photomedia, pixel abstract
Untitled 8, 2019 digital photograph with drawing
Untitled 9, 2019 digital photomedia, pixel abstract
Untitled 10, 2019 digital photomedia, pixel abstract
Untitled 11, 2019 digital photomedia, pixel abstract
Untitled 12, 2019 digital photomedia, pixel abstract
Untitled 13, 2019 digital photomedia, pixel abstract
Untitled 14, 2019 digital photomedia, pixel abstract

Notes

Day Six

1. The artwork *Beauties Captured in Time* by Chinese-Australian artist Wang Zhiyuan is referred to courtesy of the artist.

2. Ruby quotes from William Blake's 'The Sick Rose', in William Blake's *Songs of Innocence and of Experience: Showing the Two Contrary States of the Human Soul. 1789-1794* (public domain).

3. Ruby quotes from Blake's 'The Sick Rose'.

4. Ruby misquotes from Blake's 'The Sick Rose', the first line is, of course, 'O Rose thou art sick'.

5. Ruby quotes from Blake's 'The Sick Rose'.

6. Ruby mistakes Rainer Werner Fassbinder's film *Veronika Voss* for his film *The Marriage of Maria Braun*.

7. Ruby, in her recollection of the film critic's review, again mistakes Fassbinder's film *Veronika Voss* for *The Marriage of Maria Braun*.

Day Five

8. The artwork described is not an actual work. It is a fictional work of the imagination, but inspired by the works of urban Aboriginal women artists such as Fiona Foley. See: Ruth Skilbeck. 'Gazing Boldly Back and Forward: Urban Aboriginal Women Artists and New Global Feminisms in Transnational Art,' *The International Journal of the Arts in Society,* Volume 5, Issue 6, 2011, pp. 261-276.

Day Three

9. When Ruby has the memory/vision as she eats soup, and refers to two figures "A couple of k's from me," she is using the vernacular abbreviation for kilometres used conversationally in Australia.

Day Two

10. Ruby quotes from William Blake's 'The Tyger,' in *Songs of Innocence and Experience: Showing the Two Contrary States of the Human Soul.* 1789-1794.

Transports of Rapture

11. Ruby misquotes the opening lines of 'The Night Before Christmas' first published Dec. 1823, in *The Troy Sentinel,* newspaper, New York, the authorship of the poem has been disputed and it has been attributed to both Clement Clarke Moore and Henry Livingstone Jnr. The lines in the poem are: "'Twas the night before Christmas, when all through the house...'"

Antipodean Space

12. Ruby's translation (by Ruth Skilbeck) is of lines from Arthur Rimbaud's 'Les Premières Communions' (First Communions) in *Oeuvres de Arthur Rimbaud: Vers et proses: Revues sur les manuscrits originaux et les premières éditions mises en ordre et annotées par Paterne Berrichon; poèmes retrouvés* (1921) (public domain).

Desert Ruby

13. Information on Sydney graveyards, source City of Sydney website.

14. 'The Mystery of the Art of Fugue'. This section, is based on the musicology and music history chapter in *The Writer's Fugue: Musicalization, Trauma and Subjectivity in the Literature of Modernity* (Ruth Skilbeck's PhD thesis 2007).

The story that Margarita retells of J.S. Bach's unfinished fugue is in sources including Douglas R. Hofstadter's *Gödel, Escher, Bach: An Eternal Golden Braid–A Metaphorical Fugue in Minds and Machines in the Spirit of Lewis Carroll,* London: Penguin Books, 1979; and in Malcolm Boyd's *Bach*, Oxford University Press, 1983. For general information on gematria, see the Wikipedia entry. The gematria chart cited by Margarita is based on a Classical Latin gematria included by Christoph Rudolff in 1525 in his *Nimble and beautiful calculation via the artful rules of algebra so commonly called "coss".* (1525) See Ruth Tatlow's *Bach and the Riddle of the Number Alphabet,* Cambridge University Press 1997; and Malcolm Boyd's *Bach,* Oxford University Press, 1995, which includes this gematria chart, substituting I/J=9 for I=9; and U/V=20 for U=20.

Medusa

15. Ruby misquotes/misremembers Samuel Taylor Coleridge's poem 'The Rime of the Ancient Mariner' originally spelt 'The Rime of the Ancyent Marinere' in *Lyrical Ballads, with a Few Other Poems* by William Wordsworth and Samuel Taylor Coleridge, first published in 1798. Coleridge's actual lines are: 'As idle as a painted ship/Upon a painted ocean.'

Rocky Horror Show

16. Ruby quotes a line (translation by Ruth Skilbeck) from Rimbaud's poem 'Eternity' (éternité) in *Oeuvres de Arthur Rimbaud: Vers et proses: Revues sur les manuscrits originaux et*

les premières éditions mises en ordre et annotées par Paterne Ber-
richon; poèmes retrouvés (1921) (public domain).

Calling Paintings into Being

17. Ruby quotes from the opening lines of William Blake's 'Auguries of Innocence' ("To see a World in a Grain of Sand/ And Heaven in a Wild Flower/ Hold Infinity in the palm of your hand/And Eternity in an hour") first published in 1863 (public domain).

18. Ruby quotes (translation by Ruth Skilbeck) from Rimbaud's poem 'Eternity' (éternité). Margarita inadvertently speaks the second line; Ruby quotes in her translation, the remainder of the stanza of Rimbaud's 'éternité' in *Oeuvres de Arthur Rimbaud: Vers et proses: Revues sur les manuscrits originaux et les premières éditions mises en ordre et annotées par Paterne Berrichon; poèmes retrouvés* (1921) (public domain).

19. The story that Margarita retells of J.S. Bach's unfinished fugue is in Douglas R. Hofstadter, London: Penguin Books, 1979; and Malcolm Boyd, *Bach,* Oxford University Press, 1995. See Boyd, pp. 203-208.

20. Malcolm Boyd, 1995, pp. 203-208.

21. See Boyd's *Bach* (Oxford University Press, 1995), p.204.

22. The lines of poetry starting "I lost myself at tea today...." are by Ruth Skilbeck.

23. See Gilles Deleuze's essay *Coldness and Cruelty* in *Masochism,* New York, Zone Books, 1989. Deleuze writes about this in his essay, and this section is informed by his account and his references to Wanda von Sacher-Masoch (nee Aurore Rümelin), women philosophers, and masochism.

Acknowledgements

I am deeply grateful to my children, family, and friends.

The first edition of this novel was supported by a Pozible project and I extend my thanks to the crowdfunder supporters.

I am grateful to the late Glenda Adams; and to Professor Stephen Muecke, for reading and helpful comments on the early draft.

Wang Zhiyuan's artwork *Beauties Captured in Time* is referred to here with kind permission of the artist and I thank him.

Biography

Ruth Skilbeck is the author of books of fiction and non-fiction including new editions of novels in her Australian Fugue Series, *The Antipode Room* (2023) and *Sayonara Baby* (2023); and musico-literary studies book *The Writer's Fugue: Musicalization, Trauma and Subjectivity in the Literature of Modernity* (2016; 2017). After a career as a freelance journalist in Dublin, London and Sydney that included founding a media arts writing business; and later teaching journalism writing (feature writing and writing for media) at the University of New South Wales; she founded the publishing house Postmistress Press, later called Borderstream Books, and *Arts Features International* anthology journal, as editor-in-chief, contributing writer and photographer, before the pandemic.

She has been awarded grants including an Australia Council New Work; her journalism and research articles are published internationally, over time, in a range of media: from newspapers (such as *The Irish Times*); to arts periodicals (such as *POL Oxygen: International Design, Art, Architecture; Australian Art Collector; Not Only Black + White; Australian Art Review*); to journals (*Communication and Critical/Cultural Studies; International Journal of the Image; The International Journal of the Arts in Society; Journal of the Motherhood Initiative for Research and Community Involvement; Pacific Journalism Review*); to book chapter (*Cultural Studies of Rights: Critical Articulations*, Routledge); she has published poetry, short stories, and photographs.